SECOND SIGHTING

Marty M. Engle

**MONTAGE
BOOKS**

Montage Books, a Front Line Company,
San Diego, California

More **Strange Matter**™ from
Marty M. Engle & Johnny Ray Barnes, Jr.

No Substitutions

The Midnight Game

Driven to Death

A Place to Hide

The Last One In

Bad Circuits

Fly the Unfriendly Skies

Frozen Dinners

Deadly Delivery

Knightmare

Something Rotten

Dead On Its Tracks

Toy Trouble

Plant People

Creature Features

The Weird, Weird West

Tune in to Terror

The Fairfield Triangle

Bigfoot, Big Trouble

Doorway to Doom

Under Wraps

Dangerous Waters

Strange Forces

Strange Forces 2

Strange Forces 3

TO GAYE NORMAN

(IN APPRECIATION OF HER WONDERFUL DAUGHTER)

ISBN 1-56714-066-1

Printed in the U.S.A.

1

Twelve-year-old Ross Hall looked up into the blinding sweep of the spotlight and *knew* he was caught.

His blood turned to ice water. A tidal wave of terror surged through him, twisting his insides like a wet rag, squeezing out a startled gasp. He felt a fist close around his heart as his body grew rigid. He somehow managed to swallow the scream, a futile gesture since no one would ever hear him over the roar of the engines.

The light stayed on him as hurricane-force winds descended from the sky. The throbbing staccato blasts of air pressed hard against his ashen face, whipping his long brown hair and the surrounding bramble into a frenzy. He choked as the cold night air filled with clouds of dirt and debris.

For a terrifying instant, he pictured his airborne pursuers peering down at his crouched, curled form, which was only partially hidden within the scraggy bush on the sloping hillside.

The light didn't move.

Neither did he.

The single shaft of white light held him transfixed like a deer caught in headlights, its cold gaze numbing him to the core. He could scarcely feel the shaking branches and briars slashing against his face and neck under the forceful winds. Billowing clouds of dirt swirled like a snowstorm inside the glowing cone.

Still, the light didn't move.

His limbs felt as if they were on fire, his motionless body was riddled with painful cramps. He fought the urge to breathe, struggling against his frantic, empty lungs, never taking his stinging eyes off the blinding spotlight in the sky. Between stabbing pains, his brain burned with a single repetitive thought—*the slightest movement, and they will see you.*

Ross was a survivor, and no amount of pain or fear would make him give up or give in. He and his father had known this could happen.

They knew someone or something would probably come. Of course, they had never really gotten around to figuring out exactly what they'd do when it happened. The sheer excitement of anticipating the event had chased away any chance of critical thinking—or planning.

The light didn't move.

Rivulets of cold sweat poured down his fear-frozen face. Remaining motionless was truly torturous now since every survival instinct in his body screamed at him to get away—to jump up and run. Thoughtlessly. Aimlessly. Pointlessly. Suddenly, running didn't sound as dumb as before.

Then the cone of light moved.

His pupils ballooned immediately, leaving only a slight ring of brown as the light continued its sweep down the hillside, glancing off shrubs, garbage, and sandy dirt.

Ross calmed himself with a deep breath as the darkness returned. He felt a faint glimmer of hope.

Maybe they *didn't* see him.

Maybe he was better at hiding than he'd thought. Maybe they only saw branches, briars, and dirt-caked soda cans. Why else would they let their searchlight move on? They really didn't seem him. Incredible! A dumbstruck sense of triumph exploded in his brain and emerged in the form of a grim smile and a disbelieving laugh. His entire body seemed to breathe.

The feeling of relief passed quickly as his eyes followed the *path* of the light.

It drifted down the hill to the footprints his size-seven sneakers had made, illuminating the edges, making them seem as prominent as craters on the moon. His frantic mind raced, trying to decide if they could see them. How could they not? From his vantage point, the tread marks seemed as deep and as well-lit as those in photographs of the first man on the moon, Neil Armstrong. Still, with the clouds of dirt and the pitch darkness outside the spotlights . . . he supposed it was possible they didn't . . .

The light snapped back to him.

He ran.

He exploded from the bushes and ran up the hill on frantic, unsteady legs. His sneakers dug in hard, creating small avalanches of dirt and rocks.

Behind him, at the bottom of the hill, sat the forlorn, grungy mobile home he shared with his dad. For the past ten years, it'd been the only human residence in that particular twenty-mile stretch of valley. The yellow porch light was on, and the screen door was open. Inside, a television flickered like a pale blue ghost, but there was no one watching it.

Overhead, unmarked black helicopters hovered like wasps, filling the sky with searchlights and whirring blades, their positions betrayed by blinking red nose lights and small white tail lights. Their search beams swept across the roof and aluminum siding of the house, then over the cracked windshield of the dirty Ford Ranger parked haphazardly out front. Both truck doors were open, and the engine was still running.

Ross reached the top of the hill and turned back to see the first helicopter land beside the house as two others hovered nearby, monstrous silhouettes looming in the night sky.

His sneakers slid, and he struggled to regain his footing. His mouth dropped open in horror as he stared at the house in shock.

The first of the men in black uniforms sprang from the helicopter. No insignia. No signs. No badges. No arm bands.

Others followed, some signaling toward the top of the hill. They were coming after him.

Then Ross saw one of the other helicopters hovering a hundred yards behind his house. Its spotlight had stopped moving, trained on something on the ground—another target. Ross felt a lump rise in his throat and he started to tremble.

They had found his father.

Ross turned, intending to start the twenty-minute run to the main highway, never imagining it would be hours before he would make it there—where he would forever change the lives of two others.

A blinding spotlight struck him in the face, paralyzing him. Rising from behind the hill came an aerial shape of another kind. A silent kind. A carnival of colors joined the white spotlight—red, green, blue. Ross Hall's heart had merely stopped before. Now it felt as if it would explode.

Engulfed in the lights, he felt his feet rise off the ground . . .

2

6:45 pm - Feldstein Observatory

The young woman stepped to the podium with a confident, authoritative stride and scanned the fidgety audience. Her red hair, pulled back tightly in a bun, stood out in stark contrast against the white walls of the room and the mammoth telescope behind her.

The telescope, a massive tube-like frame of steel and cable, jutted through the half-dome roof, pointing at the sky through the wide opening. A railed stairway led to the control console and the eyepiece.

The woman waited patiently for the scrawny man in the front row to finish his coughing fit, and for the two little boys near the back of the room to stop their whispering.

While waiting, she casually slid her slender right hand into the pocket of her long white coat and pulled out a softly beeping pager. It was her assistant, Sheila, paging her with the regular number. Since it wasn't an emergency, Sheila could wait. Public relations was the part of her job Linda Weber enjoyed most. Since she had quit her government position, she'd gone back to her two first loves, astronomy and ufology.

"As of late December 1986 there were 7,087 man-made objects in space," she began. "Including ten screws, each an eighth of an inch in diameter, that were discarded during a 1984 shuttle mission, a thermal glove that floated out of Gemini 4 in 1965, a screwdriver lost by a space-walking cosmonaut aboard the Russian Mir Space Station, and a few thousand satellites. Some of them still work, others are nothing more than worthless junk transmitting outdated signals to stations that are no longer there. All of this heavy traffic is monitored 24 hours a day by the U.S. Space Surveillance Center at Cheyenne Mountain, Colorado. It was there, on a late December evening in 1986, on a glowing computer screen in a windowless room, that the 7,088th object was detected. Something that could not be explained."

With the exception of the two boys, everyone in the room fell silent, listening intently to her every word. Linda was very good at getting people's attention and keeping it. And, as twelve-year-old Sean Edwards would find out later, she was good at focusing that attention as well.

Sean was sitting at the back of the room next to a friend he wasn't surprised to see. A UFO lecture anywhere in the remote vicinity of Fairfield would guarantee Morgan Taylor's attendance. Morgan was the biggest UFO fanatic at Fairfield Junior High.

Morgan smiled. "She's pretty good. Nice opening bit. She's referring to an unidentified object that tripped our 'fence'."

"Huh?" Sean asked.

"A UFO tripped our electronic 'fence', a defense perimeter field in space that stretches from Georgia to Canada. It warns remote tracking stations if anything strays into our air space. Anyway, you still moving in a month?"

"Yeah," Sean replied and turned away, implying that he wanted to listen to the speaker. Morgan didn't seem to be paying much attention.

He acted as if he already knew everything she was talking about and could casually float in and out of her speech without missing a thing.

"That's gotta be pretty exciting," Morgan whispered.

" 'Exciting' is not the word I would use," Sean whispered back.

"What do you mean?" Morgan asked.

"It's not like we *want* to move. Dad has to because of his job. Bonnie's the only one excited about moving."

"Your mom, you mean?"

"Stepmom. And I mean 'Bonnie'."

"Anyway, a new town could be—"

"Morgan, I'm trying to listen."

"So am I," whispered the man sitting next to Sean. A piece of butterscotch candy rolled around in his mouth, clicking against his teeth.

"Sorry."

"We're sorry."

The man leaned back and folded his muscular arms over the small round belly that sat on his lap. Though far from paunchy, his stomach gave him the look of someone edging toward retirement. His jacket was the same color as the butterscotch candy in his mouth. He hated the color, but it was a comfortable jacket.

Wait. What was she saying? he wondered. It wasn't that he wasn't interested—he simply had other things on his mind. His short-term memory seemed to be on the verge of fading out. Another unwanted gift from the middle-age fairy. His dark brown skin was puffier than it used to be, and his closely-cropped, curly black hair was fringed with the first traces of silver. The left corner of his mouth curled up in a sea-soned sneer, perfected by years of practice.

The last of his candy dissolved on his tongue, and he found himself searching his pock-ets for another. That irritating gut kept getting in the way. When had that thing snuck up on him, anyway?

He found another piece of butterscotch, unwrapped it with surprisingly nimble fingers, and popped it into his mouth. For a moment, he wished he could give one to the guy coughing his brains out in the front row. Now, what was she saying again?

In the front row, Howard Phillips leaned forward, trying to hold the explosive force back, but failed. On more than one occasion, his coughing spells had proven to be more than an annoyance. After all, no one at a press conference had ever said, "Wait, everyone. Let's let the coughing guy finish so he can ask his question." He was convinced that his throat held some kind of grudge against him or was involved in some kind of organ conspiracy.

So, like everything else in his life that caused him grief, he had confronted the problem head-on. He visited doctor after doctor, and, after each shamefully lax examination, heard the same half-hearted answer he'd gotten before. "It's in your head, Mr. Phillips. There is no physical cause. It's simply a habit."

This, of course, infuriated him and led him to believe that all doctors were quacks. Being a reactionary as well as no small grudge-bearer, he sold his editors at *Current Edition* on the idea of producing a scathing exposé on the state of general health care. In the end, although he had gotten some personal satisfaction from writing the story, he still had the cough.

This new assignment was by far the strangest he had ever tackled. UFOs? Little green men (or as current fashion and his editors dictated, little *grey* men)? His sources had told him that there *was* something there and that he should go after it. This was his umpteenth UFO seminar in as many days and he was tired of the theorists, the conspiracy heads, and the plain old kooks. He needed something meaty. Something printable. And as he'd discovered in a routine background check, Ms. Linda Weber could possibly provide just the story he was looking for.

A few minutes later, Linda Weber finished her speech on possible alien incursion into U.S. airspace.

She then asked for questions.

Howard's hand shot up first.

"Ms. Weber? Howard Phillips from *Current Edition*. Are the stories about the so-called 'alien highways' true? Are aliens really being driven around from air force base to air force base in black sedans?"

Linda seemed a little surprised. The question had absolutely nothing to do with her lecture. "I'm sorry, but I have not personally looked into that story."

There were a few chuckles from around the room. There was a rumor going around that the local Highway 51 was one of those 'alien highways.' Morgan didn't laugh. Neither did Mr. Phillips or Ms. Weber.

Ms. Weber continued, "I would like to add, however, that stories like 'alien highways' should not be dismissed simply because they sound ridiculous. Scientifically speaking, it's often as difficult to prove that something *didn't* happen as it is to prove that it *did*. I take it by your tone, Mr. Phillips, that you regard the UFO phenomena with some disdain. I am a serious scientist, Mr. Phillips, as are my colleagues. Ufology should be regarded no differently than any other field of objective scientific inquiry."

"Uh, huh." Mr. Phillips cleared his throat with a wet rattle (the calm before the storm). "What about the wild rumors of the existence of so-called EBEs—Extraterrestrial Biological Entities who are currently guests of the United States government? In particular, of Air Force Special Intelligence and the Defense Intelligence Agency. In your opinion, is there a chance there could be something to those rumors?"

Ms. Weber didn't lose her composure. "Once again, I have not personally looked in to that particular story, but—"

Howard didn't even wait for her to finish. "You *are* Linda Weber, right? You *did* work for the DIA, did you not?"

That last part shocked her.

It shocked Marlon Walker, too. He almost choked on his butterscotch.

One of Linda's eyebrows arched, and a perturbed scowl crossed her face.

"Yes, I did."

"Well then, c'mon. Everybody's heard those stories. Surely with your interest in the subject, your expertise in the field, and your position in the DIA, these two stories must have crossed your desk at some point? Right?"

"Mr. Phillips, my interest in the existence of alien intelligence is strictly personal. My involvement with the DIA did not concern UFOs. I only dealt with the recovery and assimilation of data from downed foreign satellites inside U.S. airspace. Now, believe it or not, Mr. Phillips, there are other people who have questions."

Howard didn't buy her story, but he conceded with a loud cough as she called on the next person. His reporter's instinct told him that Linda Weber was not telling the whole truth— and although he didn't know it for certain yet, he was absolutely right.

3

After the question-and-answer session, Morgan and Sean walked around the exhibit tables. They looked at the blurry photographs, read the sworn witness affidavits, studied the alien drawings by abductees, and marveled over "official" copies of declassified secret defense documents.

Sean didn't know much about UFOs, but he was very interested in them. Morgan was trying to cram as much information as he could into Sean's head.

"Look! There's Vance's table. Vance Lewis. He's cool. He builds great models. He used to be an engineer with some big jet company. I forgot the name. They fired him for putting a jet engine into a Volkswagen Bug and testing it on one of their runways. He knows some very scary people in weird places. He's at all of these lectures. That's how I met him. Actually, if you go to enough of them, you'll start seeing the same faces over and over. It's almost like a club."

Sean believed it.

They rushed over to the tables lined with models and plastered with grey alien-head stickers.

Morgan walked up to and stood proudly by a silver flying saucer with a cut-away view. "I was a consultant on this one."

It had a domed center chamber, rounded control panels, three seats, and a standing grey alien inside. Somebody had spilled a drop of black coffee on the tiny floor.

"Hmmm. I'd go with them, that's for sure," Sean said.

"Go with whom?" Morgan asked, staring at the model with more than just a casual inter-est.

"The aliens. I would go with them if they gave me the chance."

Morgan scoffed. "Yeah, right."

"I'm totally serious."

Morgan finally realized that he was. "Why? Are you crazy?" Morgan exclaimed. His fear of the concept was very real.

"I'd go with them if it meant I didn't have to move to Elmwood."

"WHAT? Elmwood can't be that bad! Bad enough to leave your planet? Your friends? Your family?"

"Like I said, Bonnie's the only one who *wants* to go. Her family lives there. I don't want a new family, a new school, or a new house. I just don't wanna deal with it. It'd be better if aliens would come down and take me away."

"You *are* insane." Morgan stared at the drop of coffee and rubbed his nose. "I gotta go. Is your sister giving you a ride?"

"Yeah, she's around here somewhere. How about you? How are you getting home?"

"Flying, of course."

For a moment, Sean thought he was serious. "Later. See you at school."

As Morgan walked toward the stairway exit next to the telescope, he called back to Sean with a reply that would be far more prophetic than he could ever have realized.

"I'll tell you one thing, Sean. You'd better be careful what you wish for."

4

A young man with three days of stubble on his face bounded over to Sean, who was now standing alone in front of the models. The guy, wearing a battered ball cap backward and an unbuttoned, ratty flannel shirt, stopped on the other side of the table. Underneath, he wore a stained "I believe" T-shirt. He carefully blotted the coffee off the model with a rag.

"Hey, little man. What do you think of the collection?"

"Vance Lewis, right? You built these?"

"Guilty as charged. They're not for sale though, so don't even ask." He pushed his long brown hair back over his ears and smiled. "Lookin's free, though."

Sean leaned over to study the models a little more closely. There was a phaser-type gun, like on *Star Trek,* but smaller and more simple. There were models of different alien heads—from stereotypical 'greys' to near-humans with scaly skin. The most outlandish, however, was a complex model of a flying saucer that reminded Sean of a manta-ray—greyish and angry looking.

"Cool, isn't it? I built it from the actual blueprints."

Sean sniffled to show his disbelief.

"Seriously, O'-Doubting-One. My friend at Nellis snuck them out. I won't tell you how, you don't want to know. Well, okay, he hollowed out a . . ." Vance mumbled, shaking his head. "They fired him. Not over this—oh, they knew all about it, sure—but because he smarted off to one of the senior designers. Can you believe it? He went public with the whole thing, man. Saucers, treaties, contracts, alien ambassadors. I'm talking the whole nine yards. Touchdown, in the propulsion sense of the word, hear what I'm saying? We're gonna build our own, though."

"Seriously?" Sean asked with a smile.

Vance smiled too. "Seriously, man," he laughed, giving Sean a high-five. He liked this kid. Nice and—

"Hey, Mr. Walker! Haven't seen you in a while!" Vance called over Sean's head.

"Hello, Vance. How you doing?"

Sean watched the butterscotch guy saunter up—the guy who had told Morgan and him to quiet down earlier.

"Still livin'," Vance said, shaking Mr. Walker's hand. "This here's my buddy—?"

"Sean Edwards."

"Sean Edwards," Vance declared with a wave of his hand and a smile.

"Hmmm. Yes, we've met."

"Vance, are these things real? I mean, are they based on real things?" Sean asked.

"Yeah. About as real as that *Star Warriors* show or whatever thing on TV," Marlon Walker said.

Vance's eyes narrowed.

"My man, these models are 100% authentic, federally disapproved, Grade-A fabrications of everything that Big Brother doesn't want you to know about. Brought to you by Nellis Air Force Base, Plasto-Model Corp., and a few bureaucratic buddies in high but hidden places."

Sean liked Vance. He didn't know why, but he did. He got the impression that Vance wasn't much older than he was, though he had to be at least thirty. He sounded like someone who was very smart, but spoke in an odd way, as though to keep people at a safe distance—the way a rattlesnake uses its rattle.

"If the army knows that aliens and UFOs exist, why don't they want us to know about them?" Sean asked.

"Because," Linda Weber answered as she strode over, "if any evidence of alien intelligence turned out to be genuine and the public found out, it could mean major changes in everything. And it's not the army you'd have to worry about. Hi, Vance. It's so good to see you again." Vance and Linda hugged in greeting.

"This lady knows what she's talking about, my man. You listen to her. She won't steer you wrong," Vance agreed.

"What do you mean 'things would change?' *What* would change?" Sean asked.

"Some believe *everything* would change. The way we think about ourselves, our institutions, every foundation we take for granted, from banking to government. I'm sorry, but weren't you one of the little whisperers sitting in the back?"

Sean nodded, slightly embarrassed.

"What's your name?"

"Sean Edwards," he said nervously.

"Nice to meet you, Sean."

Marlon Walker cut in, offering his hand to Linda before Sean could say anything else. "Ms. Weber, I really enjoyed your lecture," he said with a warm smile. "So you were with the DIA?" He already knew the answer to that question.

"Yes. A while back. I was a burrower for General Westcott."

He smiled and reached into his pocket. "Now *there's* a thankless job. I'm Marlon Walker, and I'm with the DIA myself. Special Investigations," he said, offering her a card.

She took it, read it, then handed him one of her own. "Pleased to meet you, Mr. Walker. What brings you to my lecture? Anything in particular?"

"Oh, no. Not really," Mr. Walker said. A lie. "Just curious, I suppose. There's been so much talk recently about UFOs around here that I wanted to acquaint myself with the subject." A tremendous lie.

"Unfortunately, Mr. Walker, I'm afraid that even after ten years of acquainting myself with the subject, I don't know much more than you do."

Her pager beeped in her pocket. It had to be Sheila again. "Excuse me."

When she looked at the display, her face turned white as a sheet. A strand of red hair fell onto her suddenly sweaty forehead. The number displayed was a very special emergency number. One used only in certain circumstances. Dire ones.

"You'll have to excuse me a moment."

She practically ran to the staircase exit and vanished as the door closed behind her.

Vance looked at Marlon with disgust. "You're DIA? Man, just when you think you know a guy."

On the deserted first floor, Linda Weber opened the door to her dark office. The lights were off for a good reason.

She could barely make out the outline of the desperate person hiding in the dark, sitting in the visitor's chair in front of her desk. A person she had hoped never to meet face to face.

Her voice trembled slightly. "It's okay. I'm going to help you, but you have to trust me. I have to make a phone call."

She closed the door.

5

9:40 pm - Bloom Mountain, Highway 51

The road down to Fairfield from Bloom Mountain was long, winding, and not very pleasant. Particularly for the driver.

The passenger, on the other hand . . .

"Wow! Look at the stars!" Sean exclaimed, leaning forward and looking up through the windshield.

Millions of stars filled the sky, without any city lights to obscure them.

"Lean back! You're making me nervous. I'm trying to watch the road," Patty said, both hands firmly locked onto the steering wheel.

She wasn't kidding. A light fog covered the road, making visibility poor at best. She kept flipping the truck's headlights to high-beam, but it didn't seem to help much.

"Well, was it worth the trip?" Patty asked. "Did you have fun?"

"Yeah. I guess. I met some pretty interesting people, to say the least."

"You'll meet plenty more when we move to Elmwood," Patty said.

Silence from the passenger seat.

"Oh, Sean. Don't start. Please. Not now. It's late, I'm tired, and I have to drive."

"I'll drive," Sean quickly offered.

"Yeah, right. As if I want a ticket. Or worse, we'd end up in the bottom of the valley or stuck in a tree or something."

"Your confidence in me is truly awe-inspiring, Sis," Sean said, folding his hands behind his head.

Patty boiled. She really didn't want to talk about it again, but the seed had been planted. "You're being such a baby about this move. Dad feels bad enough, and you're making him feel worse. Not to mention what you're doing to Mom—"

"Bonnie doesn't care if I'm miserable. She just wants to be with *her* family, not ours."

"That's not true and you know it," Patty said sharply. "She has nothing to do with it. It's a corporate move. She's only trying to make things as easy as she can on us, but you make it hard. Stop calling her 'Bonnie', too. It's 'Mom' now, all right?"

"I told Morgan Taylor that I wanted aliens to come and pick me up," Sean said.

"When you're like this, I wish they would, too. Actually, I think they already did. My real brother could never be so pig-headed, selfish, and uncaring. You are obviously an alien duplicate—a plant, a fake."

Sean grinned. "Yeah. You got me. I'm just waiting for the proper time to summon my alien horde to rid the world of you pesky humans once and for all."

The fog outside was growing thicker by the moment. The shrubs and rocks on the side of the road were no longer clearly visible. The tree-tops that poked up from the sloping sides of Bloom Mountain were now merely passing shadows. Patty slowed the truck considerably.

"What are you doing? It's gonna take us forever to get home!" Sean said.

"At least we'll *make* it home. I don't want to take any chances in this soup."

"You know, that was a creepy thought."

"What was?"

"About me being an alien plant. A 'Sean duplicate.' What if that were true? What if I was waiting for the chance to strike? Waiting for a moment when you would be most vulnerable to alien inhabitation. Like right now. What if I wasn't really human, Patty?" Sean smiled wickedly, "—and you just didn't know it."

Silence.

Patty shook her head. "Very funny, Sean. Now cut it out."

Silence.

Patty frowned. "Sean. Sean?"

Patty looked over to Sean and saw his white, pupiless eyes staring at her, his mouth thrown wide open in a frozen silent scream.

"SEAN EDWARDS! You know I hate that! It's positively gross!"

He had turned his eyelids inside out and rolled his eyes back into his head. It was a very gross trick he had been doing since he was eight years old. The screaming mouth was strictly for horrific effect.

Sean laughed hysterically, then blinked his eyes back to normal. "Whoa. I must be getting old. It hurts to do that now."

Patty laughed, glancing over to Sean. Maybe she did need a little tension breaker. "I think you *are* from another planet, brother dear."

"PATTY, LOOK OUT!" Sean screamed.

But it was too late.

The figure emerged out of nowhere, standing in the middle of the road, looking like a phantom. It had a haunting face with wide eyes that glared at them through the windshield. Its mouth opened into a perfect black oval as the headlights flooded its face. It was the face of a little boy.

They were going to hit him, and there was nothing Patty could do.

6

Sean grabbed the wheel and jerked hard to the right. The world seemed to spin as the phantom figure vanished into the darkness, and the high-beams caught the glint of a steel guard rail.

Patty's scream was lost in the squeal of the tires as she slammed the brakes all the way to the floor.

The truck skidded sideways, the guard rail moving from the view out the front windshield to the driver side window. Sean clutched the door handle, ready to open the door in panic, though his seat belt still held him in place.

The truck finally stopped in a spray of gravel and a rough bump as the driver's side scraped against the guard rail.

For a moment, Patty and Sean just sat

there and breathed heavily, watching the tops of the pine trees sway in the slowly rolling fog.

Sean found the courage to speak first.

"Did—did we hit him?"

Patty tried to stop shaking but couldn't.

Her hands felt like they were permanently attached to the steering wheel.

"I don't think so. I think he got out of the way. It was a boy, Sean. A little boy! Standing in the middle of the road! Why? What was he doing there? Did I imagine it? Did you see him too?"

Sean didn't answer.

He simply watched the reflection of the boy growing closer and closer in the mirror on his side of the truck. The boy, who looked close to Sean's age, was trying to run but seemed on the verge of exhaustion. His clothes were tattered and filthy.

"H-He's coming up right behind us," Sean stammered.

Patty reached over with a shaking hand and locked her door. Sean did the same.

The boy's face appeared at Sean's window causing him to pull away with a start. The boy's eyes were crazed, wild. He looked them both over and then scanned the interior of the truck as well. His hair was matted with bits of leaves and dirt.

"C-Can you help me? Please? Can you help me?" he asked, his brow wrinkling like an old man's. His eyes filled with tears.

"What were you doing standing in the middle of the road like that? You could have been killed!"

"Can you give me a ride? I got stranded! I have to meet my dad and maybe my mom! Please! You gotta help me! Please!"

Patty looked over at Sean and bit her bottom lip. Her eyes said it all.

Sean leaned over and looked at the boy a little more intently. Maniacs come in all sizes, Sean thought. And all ages, too, probably. Still, this kid really seemed like he was in a jam. He looked as if he had just completed a marathon.

"Where is your dad?" Sean asked.

"He should be waiting at a little restaurant down the road a few miles. A place called the Al-e-inn."

Sean knew of that place. He'd never been there, but Morgan had told him all about it. It was a crummy little roadside diner, like a truck stop, that catered to the kooky crowd that hung around the observatory. It was kind of a land-mark. They had a cheap UFO museum and a space-themed menu.

"It's just down the highway, Patty. We'll pass it on the way home."

"Maybe he could ride in the back," Patty whispered.

"Patty! Look at him—he's just a kid. He's scared to death, and it'll be cold back there."

"I'm going to regret this," she mumbled, as he opened his door and climbed out to let their new passenger aboard.

The red Toyota pickup turned around and continued down the mountain.

"What's your name?" Sean asked.

"Ross. Ross Hall."

High above them, a dark shadow passed through the night sky, blocking out the stars, gliding in absolute silence.

Its ominous shadow fell on the truck and kept pace, undetected.

7

What a dump. Why did I stop here? Marlon thought to himself. I must be a glutton for punishment. He took another spoonful of soup and another swig of black coffee. He kept staring at a photograph hanging over the milkshake machine, one of a long line of them on the diner's walls. It was a picture of a silver disc hovering high in the sky over a mailbox standing near some power lines.

"Excuse me. Where was that picture taken?" he asked the beefy man with the rolled-up shirt sleeves and the hound-dog face. The man didn't look up from his task of wiping the counter with a folded white rag.

"My house."

34

"Oh," Marlon smiled. "Did you take it yourself?"

"Yes, I did."

Not much of a conversationalist, thought Marlon, raising his eye brows.

Looking around, he didn't think he could strike up a chat with *anyone* in the place. He was the only person at the counter, and the few locals in the booths kept staring at him. He felt as if he would have been more welcome if he had been from another planet.

He took another spoonful of soup as a tall skinny man in overalls walked out of the narrow hallway that led to the restrooms. He could still hear the toilet flushing as the man passed the counter, staring at him from the corner of his eyes all the while.

He looked from the man to the small roped-off diorama of the Al-e-inn's re-creation of the famous Roswell crash of 1947. An aluminum foil saucer sat in front of a poorly painted background mural of the desert. Four paper-maché aliens were lying under it in various positions.

"Nice scene. You build it yourself?"

"Yeah." The man didn't look up. He just turned his rag over and continued wiping.

Marlon ran his tongue across his teeth and wished again that he hadn't run out of butterscotch candies. He rubbed the back of his neck and then pulled a small laptop computer from his briefcase.

The man abruptly stopped wiping the counter and his eyes shot wide open upon seeing the computer. He backed away as if Marlon had pulled a gun.

"Just gotta get a little work done," Marlon laughed. "Wish they'd never invented these portables."

The man didn't say a word.

This was not helping Marlon's mood. He was already tense and edgy from the seminar and lying to Linda Weber. He really liked her and thought she was an excellent speaker. Any hope that she could shed some light on his problem had vanished when she'd disappeared after getting that message on her pager. No one had seen her for the rest of the event.

Marlon didn't like this place. The entire front wall, including the door, was covered with closed blinds. He'd never felt such intense paranoia coming from the people around him, and for a Defense Intelligence Agency operative, that was a real statement.

These people obviously have a problem with government officials, he thought. He supposed they had seen his license plates and were trying to figure out exactly who he was working for.

He'd met their type before—paranoids who were terrified of men in black suits, driving black cars, flying black helicopters, showing up at their doors and telling them to keep quiet about what they had seen—or else. The infamous "Men-in-Black" or "MIBs" as they were called in popular UFO stories.

These kooks would absolutely freak if they knew that at that very moment there was an official, card-carrying MIB sitting in their midst, eating soup while looking up the list of people he had to "visit" next.

It was no joke.

He'd lost track of the number of people he'd visited—and not once had he worn a black suit. He usually wore his Air Force Intelligence uniform, the one he was given before getting snagged by the DIA. He really didn't like what he was doing. He didn't like going to people's homes and businesses, urging them not to talk about what they had seen for the sake of national security, playing on their sense of duty to their country, scaring them half to death.

What got to him the most was the fact that *he* didn't even know what they had seen!

He only told them what he was ordered to tell them. Like everyone else in the field, he basically read a script. Of course he had his own theories. His favorite was that these people had seen flights of classified planes, like the B-2 when it was a secret, or the new Aurora spy plane. Maybe, as he had hoped Linda Weber might confirm, they had seen falling defense satellites or secret space junk. He didn't know.

He had never seriously considered UFOs before. He didn't believe in that nonsense. People in his department laughed at anyone who even brought up the subject. The official position of the DIA was evident in the joke security posters hung all over the offices—a little green man with antennae in a cartoon saucer smashing into a filing cabinet. The caption read:

Security is no accident!

Maybe he was feeling the mounting guilt of all the people he'd scared silent over the years. The fact that he never got involved with them or knew them personally made it easier, but it was a thin dike holding back a flood of frustration. Those were sane, rational people. Not kooks. Not like *this* bunch. He'd visited doctors, lawyers, judges, even a congressman or two. He'd never forget what one judge from New York had said when he opened the door and saw him standing there. "You're here because of the flying saucer I saw last night, right?"

Flying saucers. Marlon stared at the photograph again. What were these people seeing? How could he be so close to the whole mess for so long and not know a thing?

The names of the people for next week's visits began scrolling down his screen. In a moment, he would look more closely at the list— and his whole world would turn upside down.

8

10:15 pm - Highway 51

It was silent inside the truck for a few long minutes. The sound of the heater was the only noise in the cab.

At first, they had tried to get Ross to tell them how he had wound up in the middle of the highway, how he had gotten so dirty, and how he had gotten stranded up there.

Silence was their only answer

Then they had tried to find out where he lived and why he was meeting his dad at such a weird place so late at night.

Silence again.

After a few more minutes, Sean gave up. He started babbling to fill the void, telling Ross his entire life story. He rambled on about their stepmother, about how they had to move, about how terrible his father's company was for making them move, and so on.

Patty tried to shut him up a couple of times, then tried to change the subject. Ross didn't say anything. He just sat there staring at Sean in a daze. Fine. She'd let Sean ramble. It was better than silence, she supposed.

She just wanted to drop Ross at the restaurant and get home as fast as possible She'd been spooked enough for one evening.

How she'd been talked into giving Sean a ride to the lecture was beyond her. He'd been talking about going to this thing for weeks but when their stepmom offered to drive him, he seemed to lose interest. Finally, Bonnie decided it would be best if Patty drove him. Anything to cheer him up and get his mind off the move.

It isn't like Sean is a bad kid or anything, Patty thought. He's just having a lot of problems adjusting to our new situation.

She still wasn't sure why Sean was blaming everything on Bonnie. Maybe it was just the easiest thing to do. He'd told her once, on the verge of tears, that he felt like just when things were going great for him—just when he was comfortable—he was being forced to start all over again in a brand new town, and there wasn't anything he could do about it. That's when he had started talking about getting picked up by aliens. Not surprising. He was really into science fiction. One trip to his room proved that. He had even painted a sign and hung it on his bedroom door for everyone to see.

Aliens: Free human specimen. Take one!

They all hoped that once the family had moved and was settled in, he'd revert back to the same old Sean.

Ross just stared at Sean the entire time he was talking.

Either Sean didn't notice, or he didn't care. He was venting, and it was nice to have someone new listen to him, even if it *was* some weirdo kid they had picked up in the middle of nowhere.

He would have continued, too, but Ross finally spoke.

"I have a stepmother, too."

Sean stopped rambling.

"Really? Then you kinda know what I'm

talking about, huh?"

"No. I love my stepmother. I wish she, my dad, and I could move away like you're doing."

Sean didn't say anything. He was too stunned at the bluntness of the remark, and perhaps a bit embarrassed as well.

"Is she waiting at the restaurant, too?" Patty asked.

Ross didn't say anything for a moment. He seemed to be choosing his words.

"I don't know. I hope so." His eyes were filled with fear and dread.

Sean and Patty looked at their strange passenger and didn't say another word.

Up ahead, they saw the flash of a neon sign that read "Al-e-inn."

Marlon looked at the list of names again, hoping he had read it wrong. No such luck. There they were, big as life, in glowing green letters.

Sean Edwards. Patricia Edwards.

Sean Edwards, from the lecture. The little boy he had just met. The one who had been whispering during Linda Weber's speech. Patricia must be the girl he had left with. His sister, more than likely.

Marlon sighed heavily and rubbed the back of his head. Whatever it was Sean had seen, it had to have been after the seminar, just a few hours ago! The list was fed via satellite and updated every two minutes. He had checked it before he went into the observatory. What could those kids have possibly seen?

Another prompt appeared with a special note. It was a call for the apprehension of a person named Ross Hall. A twelve-year-old boy. He was last seen near Route 2 off of Highway 51.

Terrific. This stupid restaurant was on Highway 51, the so-called alien highway. Route 2 was not even a real road, and was only about twenty miles away. The retrieval of the boy was top priority. At least it would be if he had been on duty. He kept forgetting it was his night off. Sean Edwards, Ross Hall. More kids. Poor kids.

The badge in his jacket pocket felt heavier by the second. He suddenly had a very bad feeling about the rest of the evening.

No way, he told himself. He wasn't going to get involved. He was feeling bad enough, and besides, it was his night off.

Out front, a red Toyota truck pulled into the parking lot and parked beside his Chevy van.

<u>9</u>

10:35 pm - Al-e-inn, Highway 51

The truck's headlights switched off, and the engine stopped.

Sean jumped out and held the door as Ross slowly climbed out, looking around nervously.

"Thank you for the ride," he said, "but I don't think you should go in."

"But—" Sean started.

"We're going home, anyway. Get in, Sean. Let's go," Patty said.

Sean stood there and watched Ross stumble toward the door without another word.

"Sean. He's here. He'll find his dad. Let's go! Move it!" Patty said.

Sean looked at the strange restaurant,

particularly at the cool UFO painted on the roof with the word "WELCOME". He liked the warm flash of the neon sign.

He read the intriguing hand-painted words on the door:

"SEE! An actual re-creation of the Roswell crash with authentic replicas of alien bodies!"

Cheesy, but cool. He had heard of this place so many times, and now here it was, right in front of him.

"Sean?" Patty asked. She didn't like the look in her brother's eyes.

Then there is our mystery guest, Sean thought. What if his dad isn't in there? What if he's still stranded? This place looks kinda rough, and it's very late. Maybe Ross still needs our help. After all, we almost killed him. I have to at least make sure he has a ride home.

"Sorry, Sis, but I gotta go!"

Sean sprinted toward the door.

"SEAN EDWARDS!" Patty yelled, as she jumped out of the truck and ran after her brother.

With his heart pounding in his throat, Ross walked past the diorama and the calendar-of-events board and scanned the booths for the person or people he was supposed to meet. No sign of them anywhere.

He noticed Al, the owner, standing behind the counter.

Al Clemens' heart sank at the sight of Ross. When he saw the state of Ross' clothes and the look in the scared little boy's eyes, he knew exactly what had happened and why Ross was there. Al had known Ross' father for more years than he could count, and his stepmother for the past two years.

He found himself saying the words that broke his heart.

"They're not here, Ross."

Ross looked around anyway, searching for any sign of his father, though he knew it was futile. It had been hours since they were separated. If they weren't here by now, they never would be. Tears began to well in his eyes. His breathing quickened and his pulse raced.

"I'm sorry, Ross," Al murmured.

Sean and Patricia had just run through the doorway when two shiny black sedans pulled into the parking lot.

Sean felt something stir inside of him as

he watched Al go over to Ross and put his arm around the boy's shoulder. Obviously Ross' father and stepmother weren't here. But so what? So they were a little late. Was that anything to get so upset about?

He was fooling himself. Somehow he knew that the fact that they weren't there was a very bad thing indeed. He was about to go over to Ross when a sharp voice stopped him.

"Sean!"

"Mr. Walker?" Sean asked, surprised to see his new acquaintance again so soon. "What are you doing here?"

"I can't believe you're here!" At first, Marlon thought it was luck—but then again, he didn't believe in luck. "Is that your sister . . . Patricia?"

Sean nodded.

"Sean, come here. We gotta talk," he said, turning off his computer.

Billy Ray Williams pulled his pickup into the parking spot next to one of the shiny black sedans, being extra careful not to bang his door into its side. He came here almost every night, yet he had never seen that car here before.

He pushed the bill of his red cap up as he sauntered toward the front door of his favorite restaurant. He stretched and yawned, popping his back as he stepped over the yellow concrete slab lying at the front curb.

Eight pairs of eyes watched him from behind tinted glass as he scratched the back of his head and lazily pushed through the glass door.

Marlon lowered his voice. "Sean, have you seen anything strange tonight? Anything at all?" Marlon's voice had an urgency to it that was frightening.

"No. Well, except for Ross," he said.

Again, Marlon's heart flipped over in his chest. "Ross. Who's Ross?"

Sean pointed to the trembling boy being led to the bathroom by the man from behind the counter. Ross, in turn, was pointing Sean and Patricia out to Al.

"Him," Sean said with some confusion. "We gave him a ride. His name's Ross Hall—"

Marlon's mouth dropped open.

After the door closed behind him, Billy Ray sprinted to the counter, where he promptly announced to everyone—

"OKAY, PEOPLE! There are two carloads of MIBs out there in the parking lot! Somebody must've seen something they shouldn't have!"

At first, Marlon Walker was sure the lightning strike of pain in his chest was a heart attack. Then he realized it was only the biggest rush of adrenaline he'd had in a long time.

In an instant, he headed toward the door to see exactly who was outside, and to find out whether or not he was still off-duty.

Al silently gestured for Sean and Patricia to follow him and Ross quickly.

Ross gestured for them to run—and to run FAST!

They stood there for a second, completely confused, then sprinted.

Together Ross, Sean, Patricia, and their guide vanished into the hallway leading to the restrooms.

Marlon reached for the door, but someone beat him to it. It opened so quickly, it almost hit him in the face.

He found himself staring wide-eyed at a man in a black suit with a black hat and a black tie. Three others were coming in right behind him.

"Excuse me, sir. Did you see a twelve-year-old boy come in here?"

Marlon thought for a long moment before he answered.

"No," he said with a slight tremble. "No, I haven't seen any kids."

Al replaced the panel in the men's restroom and checked the seams to make sure it looked like one solid wall again. When he was satisfied, he shot to his feet with a loud pop, flushed the toilet, and turned out the light. He wiped his forehead as he started back through the hall toward the dining room.

There should have only been one scared kid down in the tunnel beneath the restaurant.

But now there were three.

10

The room was about the size of a large closet. It wasn't very comfortable. A string of Christmas lights on the wall of the tunnel had led them to it.

In the dim light of a hanging bulb, Sean could make out an old mildewed sofa, a cobweb-covered table, and a couple of folding chairs. There were a few cases of soda, a couple of jugs of water, and some old newspapers. A phone was hung on the wall near the door. Sean decided it was either a bomb shelter or a very bad employee break room.

Ross had the phone in his hand, but was afraid to dial. He had come so far, yet now he was afraid to make a simple phone call. Actually, it *wasn't* a simple phone call. It was a phone call that could possibly end his quest right there—and very unsuccessfully at that.

His dad trusted the person he was about to call. That's why his dad had gone to her when he realized they were all going to get caught. Ross, however, didn't know if he trusted her at all.

"What are we doing? Why are we hiding in a cellar? We didn't do anything! Who's upstairs? The police? The FBI? What did you do, you little weirdo?" Patricia demanded, on the verge of a minor breakdown herself.

"They're no one you've ever heard of," Ross mumbled, closing his eyes, trying to decide. The curly phone cord bounced in the air, leading to the black box on the wall. "No one you want to meet."

"They're Men-in-Black? Like that guy said? The MIBs? For real?" Sean couldn't decide if he should be scared or excited, so he settled on both. Real intrigue! Could that possibly mean—

"YOU SAW A FLYING SAUCER?" Sean blurted.

Ross nearly dropped the phone.

"You don't get it! You have no idea how deep you're in now, do you?" Ross snapped angrily. "This is for real. Those guys are up there and they're really looking for me . . . and the two people who helped me escape."

"Escape?!" Patricia exclaimed. "Escape from what? You were in the middle of nowhere! We almost hit you! We picked you up out of kindness—or maybe it was stupidity!"

"I told you not to come into the restaurant."

Patricia shot an angry glance at Sean, who shrugged his shoulders.

Sean's mind was racing, trying to put it all together. The MIBs are real. Does that mean UFOs are real, too? Flying saucers? Dare I hope—aliens? He saw the sign on his bedroom door take on a whole new meaning. A *real* meaning. Perhaps Elmwood wasn't his next destination after all.

"They're gonna throw us into a federal penitentiary!" Patty cried.

"Will you both be QUIET?! I'm trying to think!" Ross yelled.

He exhaled deeply and walked over to the black box. He held a business card up in the dim light and dialed the number with a shaking finger.

Sean and Patty both quieted down immediately not so much out of courtesy, but because they wanted to hear what Ross was saying into the phone.

"Hi. It's me . . . Yes . . . Yes . . . I'm there now . . . No, I don't know where he is, and I'm very scared . . . Yes."

Ross turned and faced them, unconcerned about them overhearing anything (they were in the same predicament as he was, after all).

His face lit up with a sudden flash of hope when the voice on the other end of the line said that his stepmother was fine and was waiting for him. He simply had to go meet her and everything would be settled.

"Thank you . . . for everything," Ross said, then hung up the phone.

He turned back in time to see a man enter the room, holding up a badge.

"Federal agent. You're all in a lot of trouble."

"Mr. Walker! How'd you—?"

"The owner—Al, I guess?—got the hint that I was with you and tipped me off about the tunnel. You Ross Hall?"

Ross felt rage sweep through his body. He nodded, fighting back the impulse to make a break for it.

"You have a lot of fans upstairs, young

man. Guys with boring taste in clothes. They're looking for you, and it looks like they mean business. Do you know what it's about?"

"Yes."

"Would you like to clue me in?"

"No."

"Let me rephrase that." Marlon pulled a pair of handcuffs from his jacket. "Federal agent. Now clue me in."

"Who do you work for? Which branch and department?" Ross asked.

Marlon arched his brows in surprise. This was a very weird kid. Normally, people couldn't remember their own names when confronted by a federal agent. This kid actually asked which branch.

"DIA. Special Investigations."

Ross breathed in relief, his shoulders lowering. "Then I have something for you."

Ross stepped forward and handed Marlon the business card he had been holding, the one with the number he had dialed.

"What is this?"

"I'm in a lot of trouble."

"That I surmised. You're on every snag list in Washington."

57

"I know what you do. I know how you go around to people who . . . see things. You make them keep quiet."

"I ask them to comply out of duty to their country," he snapped angrily. "I don't have to justify myself to a kid!"

"You don't even know what it is they've seen, do you?"

Marlon didn't say anything.

"If you help me get to my stepmother, I'll tell you exactly what it is they've seen."

Marlon couldn't believe he was hearing this from a kid. He *really* couldn't believe what he asked in reply.

"Where is your stepmother?"

"She's with the person on that card. The person who's gonna help me. She can help you, too. She can answer a lot of questions."

Marlon looked down at the card and wasn't a bit surprised. He supposed he should've been, but he wasn't.

He wasn't exactly sure who was roaming around upstairs, guarding all the exits, even patrolling the skies in black helicopters, of all things. But he knew they weren't DIA, and he wasn't too eager to turn these kids over to them.

Finally, it was the name on the card that made him agree.

The name: Linda Weber.

11

The tunnel, Ross informed them, had been built in the fifties as a tornado shelter. In the sixties, it was a bomb shelter. In the seventies and eighties, it would have served as a hiding place had the civilized world collapsed, and now in the nineties, it was there in the event an alien horde invaded the restaurant.

The restaurant had been invaded all right, but the horde wasn't exactly alien.

"I can't believe we made it!" Sean said, still breathless with excitement. The MIBs, flying saucers, federal agents, and now a mysterious scientist. Incredible. All this made his other troubles seem a million light years away. Elmwood? Who cares about Elmwood and Bonnie? The way things are going, I could very well be on my way to another planet tonight!

"Just be glad they didn't check my plates," Marlon said. Deep down, he figured they had, but decided not to question him further for some reason. Or maybe they really *hadn't* run a check on his tags. If they hadn't, they were pretty sloppy. They should have ID'd every car in the parking lot. After leaving the kids in the tunnel, he'd simply flushed the toilet, walked back into the diner, picked up his stuff, gotten in his car, and left.

Simple as that.

The mile-long drive to the drainage ditch where the tunnel emerged had been easy enough. The kids snuck into his Chevy van without a helicopter in sight.

"Do you think those guys will catch up to us? Do you think they're tailing us now?!" Sean asked Marlon, poking his head between the front seats like a kid going on vacation, pestering his parents to see if they were almost there.

"They aren't bad guys, Sean. They're just guys doing their jobs. Like me. Or like I used to do until I pulled *this* stunt," he moaned, shaking his head. "They did the same thing I was going to have to do."

"What do you mean?" Sean asked.

"You were on my list. You and Patricia,"

he said, checking the rear view mirror.

"You're a MIB, too? You were going to come after us, like they did Ross? Why? It's not like we saw a flying saucer or anything! Even if we had, what gives you the right to tell us to keep quiet about it? Man, just when you think you know a guy." Sean leaned back, both upset and disappointed.

"It's not that way at all. Look, do you think the DIA cares if people go around claiming they saw flying saucers or flying cigars or whatever? Do you think we'd care if you went to the papers with your story? We don't care. No one would believe you. You'd be just another kook with a kooky UFO story. But, if you made a loud enough stink, *other* people might believe you. People like the FBI, the CIA, or AFSI . . ."

"Or the DIA," Sean said snottily.

"Or the DIA. We're all human. We're all trying to get to the bottom of these mysterious sightings in case they pose a threat to the country. But we wind up getting in each other's way—start holding out on each other—hiding evidence for ourselves because we all want to be the first to solve the mystery. Then we can control the information and how it's utilized. Pretty soon, it's impossible to get any answer because everyone only has a small piece of the puzzle, and no one's sharing. See what I mean?"

"Yeah. I think so," Sean said.

"So you see, by keeping situations quiet, we can come in, do our investigation, and not rock any other boats."

"Only it doesn't always work?"

Marlon had to smile. Sean's a smart kid. It *never* worked. That's why there are still over 200,000 unsolved cases of unidentified aerial phenomena.

He changed the subject. "Those guys back at the restaurant? You know what? They probably have sons and daughters like you."

"It still doesn't give them the right to break up families," Ross said.

After that, they rode in silence until they reached the observatory.

And a betrayal.

12

11:10 pm - Feldstein Observatory

Linda was waiting out front when they pulled through the open gate of the electric fence. They parked beside her Honda Civic in front of the main entrance to the observatory. The large half-dome of the telescope atrium loomed above them like an earthbound half-moon. The real moon, glowing bright blue, seemed small in comparison.

She held a pale hand up to her face as the headlight beams washed over her then died.

Ross was the first one out of the van. He ran to Linda as fast as he could.

"Ross, she's inside. She's fine."

Ross clutched Linda around the waist and hugged her as hard as he could, but only for a moment. He ran up the concrete steps to the glass and steel entrance of the reception area and vanished inside. The blinds covering the windows and door were shut tightly.

"Mr. Walker . . . and company. I'm surprised to see you again so soon," she said, clutching her arms and trying to stay warm as Marlon, Sean, and Patricia closed the van doors. "It's very fortunate that you got to Ross first. When I heard the news, I feared someone other than the DIA would get to him."

"Lucky accident. Lucky for him, anyway. Would you like to tell me what's going on? Like how you know that kid?"

"And why Patricia and I are on the MIBs' most wanted—" Sean said.

Marlon interrupted, "And why Ross' family is the hottest thing around besides the sun— or are you going to give me a line about how I know about as much as you do?"

She smiled. "Come inside. There's someone you should meet."

Their footsteps echoed on the marble floor as they walked through the main hall. The lights were off, and the antiseptic white walls and floor glowed blue in the moonlight.

"I was a burrower for a long time, Mr. Walker. You know what they say about burrowers."

Marlon interjected. "One good burrower is worth a hundred good field operatives."

"What's a burrower?" Sean asked.

Linda smiled. "A burrower is someone who sits alone at a table in the National Archives in Washington, D.C. or Suitland, Maryland, until three or four every morning. They pour over thousands and thousands of documents to glean out those little bits of real information that make or break unsolved cases."

"If that information is so important, why don't they keep it in better order? Why do you have to dig through a bunch of stuff to find anything?" Patricia asked.

Mr. Walker answered, "That goes back to what we were talking about before. About how everyone tries to keep stuff to themselves. Well, sometimes false documents or inaccurate reports are created to help do that. It's called disinformation and it makes it a real pain to get to the truth of a situation sometimes. That's why burrowers are so important. The DIA has about

50,000 burrowers at work every day."

"I understand your frustration, Mr. Walker. That's why I'm talking to you. I had the same problem you have now, but on the opposite end. I was digging through documents pertaining to the types of situations they were sending you into the field to control. I couldn't make heads or tails of anything, either. They weren't giving me enough information. I, along with many others, were told where to dig, what to dig for, and for how long to dig. Decentralized information gathering. Many burrowers get the pieces of crucial information they need, but no one gets enough to put together the whole puzzle. No one but the heads of the intelligence agencies ever know the whole truth."

"The truth, the whole truth, and nothing but the truth, as long as it isn't all in once place for anyone to get to."

"Exactly."

"So, at the lecture this evening, you knew who I was all along?"

"Yes."

"Man, just when you think you know someone."

"Mr. Walker. Sean. Patricia. I'd like you to

meet Kira."

Under the dark mammoth telescope poking through the open skylight of the half-dome roof of the observatory, two figures were seated on the steps, huddled close together.

One was a small boy.

The other, a woman.

The first thing Sean noticed was an odd glow coming from the woman. It was very faint, but still noticeable.

She and Ross stood and then walked over to them, hand in hand.

The closer she came, the faster Patricia's heart began to beat.

The closer she came, the more tense Mr. Walker grew.

She walked up to Sean, who was absolutely petrified—frozen in place by fear and excitement. Suddenly, everything he had always half-joked about and half-wished for was standing right in front of him.

The woman was obviously not human!

Her forehead was unusually high, framed by long brownish-blonde hair. Her body seemed human, extremely thin and feminine. She wore jeans, boots, and a light-blue denim shirt. Her eyes were larger than a human's but only slightly, and were a brilliant violet color. Her mouth and nose seemed perfectly normal. It was her skin that betrayed her otherworldly origin.

At first glance, Sean thought, she simply had a deep tan. On closer inspection, however, he realized she had *two* skins.

One was an almost transparent veil, a shimmery sheet like thin plastic. Beneath it were thousands of tiny scales like *honeycombs,* little pocketed cells of tan flesh. And they were moving, each opening and closing slightly like the gills of a fish.

"Kira," Linda said, placing a hand on the alien's shoulder. "I'd like you to meet Mr. Marlon Walker, Mr. Sean Edwards, and Ms. Patricia Edwards. They are largely responsible for your stepson being here."

"Thank you all," the alien said. Her voice sounded like several voices speaking at once, each at a different pitch. "I don't know how I can ever repay you for your help."

Marlon's eyes were the size of saucers. He tried to answer, but couldn't. He just nodded his head weakly instead.

Patricia asked the obvious, "Are—Are you

an alien?"

"I prefer the term 'off-world guest', but yes, I am. I have been here for three years. Three wonderful years. Well—" she hugged Ross' shoulders, "two wonderful years, anyway."

Marlon's cheeks puffed up like balloons and he exhaled ten years worth of built-up anxiety. His mind frantically tried to accept what he was seeing, but couldn't. It was true! It was all true! All those people. All those sightings. All these years. It was too much. He felt dizzy and nauseous.

Sean touched her hand and then recoiled as if he'd touched a snake.

"I'm sorry."

"It's okay," she replied.

"I just had to be sure, you know, that this is real."

"I assure you, Sean. I'm very real."

Marlon noticed it first.

"Do you hear something?" he asked, holding his hand up as if he would get better reception that way.

Linda looked up and saw a black helicopter fly past the open skylight, its red lights blinking in short bursts.

"No," Marlon whispered.

Linda smiled.

"No. NO!" Ross cried. "YOU LIED TO ME! YOU CALLED THEM! YOU TOLD THEM WHERE WE WERE! THEY'RE GOING TO TAKE HER, JUST LIKE THEY TOOK DAD! YOU LIED!" Ross started to panic, anger twisting his face into a red rage.

Linda was unaffected. She put her hand on Ross' shoulder and could practically feel the heat. "Ross, listen to me. We need to talk with them. We need to hear what they have to say. I was once one of them. They really are good people. They only want what's best for everyone involved. There are many aspects of this situation that you're not thinking about. They will *not* break up your family. We'll talk with them and sort this all out like rational, civilized individuals."

"Why should I trust you?" Ross asked, tears welling in his eyes.

Kira said nothing, but kept holding his hand. She had obviously discussed this with Linda before they'd arrived.

"I only want what's best for the situation, Ross," Linda said.

Ross looked at his stepmother, who nodded

in agreement. "We can't keep running, Ross. They have your father."

Marlon Walker looked from the black helicopters in the sky to Linda.

"You didn't tell them she's here. They don't know she's here at all, do they?"

"Let's go," she said with absolute confidence. "They're waiting."

It was the last time she would say anything with absolute confidence.

13

Linda and Ross stepped from the door into the glare of headlights coming from four black sedans. A voice greeted them from the bottom of the front steps.

"Hello, Ross. You can call me Kelly. It's a girl's name, I know, but I have to live with it," a smooth-voiced man laughed. His voice was soft and gentle. His smile was warm, and was topped by a bushy, well-groomed brown moustache. "How you doing, son? You all right? The thing is, I don't want you to be scared here, see? We're all on the same team, know what I mean? Apparently, some people overreacted and did you and your family a great disservice. And for that, I certainly apologize. The last thing anyone wants here is a mess, but that's what it looks like we've got, don't you think?"

Ross didn't say anything. He was glued to Linda's side. With the lights in his face, he had a hard time making out exactly how many MIBs were there. He could only feel their stares.

"Linda? How you doing? You all right?" Kelly asked.

"I'm fine. I think we're just a little scared is all. Why don't we talk about Richard Hall?" Linda suggested, holding one hand up to shield her eyes from the glare. The other rested gently on Ross' back.

"Well, he's fine, Ross. He was asking about you. Wanted to make sure you were all right and everything. He said to tell you he loves you and that he can't wait to see you—and your stepmom again. That's what we want, too, Ross. You believe me, don't ya? We all just need to get together and talk about this thing. Okay? What'd ya say, partner? Why don't you take us to your stepmom and then we'll go see your dad. Get you guys back together like it should be."

Ross didn't say anything.

Marlon didn't say anything either.

He didn't know this Kelly guy, but he knew the tone—and the routine.

He, Sean, Patricia, and Kira waited inside, safely out of sight behind the blinds near the door. Kira seemed as anxious as Marlon. He sensed that she, too, didn't completely trust the situation.

"Hey, Linda?" Kelly asked politely. "Why don't you bring Ross down here and we'll get this show on the road. I think we'd *all* like to resolve this situation and go home."

"What do you think, Ross?" Linda asked, gently nudging him.

"I think he's LYING!" Ross screamed, turning to run back inside.

More lights exploded onto the front of the building.

Linda grabbed for Ross as Kelly yelled, "Move in! Grab the kid!"

The MIBs were shocked to see a man in a tan jacket burst through the door, pulling the boy back through the now open doorway behind him. He was holding a badge high in his free hand.

"DIA!" he yelled.

His response was a cold blue blast of light—a rope-thick beam that blew a hole in the glass behind him!

"DIA! I'M DIA!" he yelled again as he

dodged down the steps and joined Linda behind her car.

Another volley of blue blasts sliced through the air, destroying the front of the building in an ear-splitting rain of glass and smoke.

Inside, Ross, Kira, Sean, and Patricia scrambled away from the doors and windows as fast as they could. They headed back to the telescope room.

Marlon and Linda huddled as another volley of blue light began blowing holes in her car as if it was made of paper.

"WHERE'D THEY GET THOSE THINGS?!" he yelled.

"Take these keys! Go through the observatory. Take the white van in the garage. Go!" Linda urged.

Marlon felt the keys slapped into his hand. He looked at her, looked at the door, then nearly caught a laser beam in the ear. He yanked his head back, certain he saw smoke come off his nose.

"GO!" Linda yelled, grabbing his arm. "Marlon, I'm sorry."

Marlon took a deep breath and sprinted up the stairs, diving through the shattered front window frame. He crouched low as sporadic rounds of fire shot through the room, filling it with an eerie blue glow.

He saw the others at the far end of the hall, entering the main telescope room. As he took off running again, his aching gut told him he should never have discovered butterscotch candy.

Linda stood up behind her car and scowled ferociously. She walked away from the piece of Swiss cheese that had once been her Honda, and past a hunk of twisted metal that used to be Marlon's van.

The MIB team ignored her. They charged into the building after their prey, armed with weapons that looked nearly identical to Vance's model phaser.

"Light pursuit! LIGHT PURSUIT!" Kelly yelled into his headset. "Make it look real! Take out the DIA if you get the opportunity."

Linda walked straight up to Kelly, who was listening to a helicopter report.

"You lied to me!"

"Sorry it went down the way it did," he wheezed. "But it's like we said, he's gonna lead us to her one way or the other."

A black sedan with a gold seal on the license plate rolled forward, the puncture-proof tires crunching on the broken glass.

Linda walked up to a rear side window as it rolled down with a sigh.

"They took off, and I don't blame them. They stole the only van here, and now I have no car," she said with as much control as she could muster.

The shadowy figure in the car gestured for Kelly. He came over and bent into the window as the man whispered.

Kelly stood back up and handed Linda the keys to a black sedan.

"Low mileage, in-deck CD, and it's all gassed up," Kelly remarked with a smile.

Linda didn't think it was funny.

The small pursuit unit moved slowly, allowing plenty of time for their prey to make it downstairs. They were ordered to move them along, but not engage them in any way.

The team passed through the main telescope area with their weapons drawn, but under orders not to shoot anyone.

They made it to the bottom of the metal exit stairs in time to hear the screeching of wheels on pavement.

They watched the vanishing tail lights of the white van as it roared onto an unmarked gravel access road.

The leader pulled his throat mike closer and said, "The pigeons have flown the coop!"

Then he smiled.

14

"Did we lose them?" Sean asked frantically, bouncing all over the front passenger seat as they sped down the extremely bumpy road.

Marlon checked the rear view mirror again. Nothing there. Only an uneven, jittering view of a gravel road and a lot of dust clouds.

"Yeah. Yeah, I guess we did," he said, though he wasn't completely convinced. It had been way too easy. They had let them go. There wasn't a single helicopter around. No whirring blades. No sweeping lights. Nothing. Absolutely nothing. And there had been very few MIBs chasing after them in the observatory. It was like they *wanted* them to escape. Of course, they didn't know Kira was there. They didn't know Sean and Patricia were with them, either. As far as they knew, it was only Ross and himself.

"Homing pigeons. They're playing us for homing pigeons," Marlon said.

"What do you mean?" Patricia called from one of the box-filled back seats. The van had no windows other than those in the rear doors, front doors, and the windshield. It had the observatory logo decal on the sides in big red letters.

Kira and Ross sat together across from Patricia.

"I mean, they let us go thinking we'll head straight for wherever Kira's been hiding," Marlon said.

"What do you think they're gonna do?" Sean asked.

"They're not going to attack again, that's for sure. They want us to think they're long gone. They won't do anything until they're 100% convinced they know where we're going."

"So what *are* we going to do?" Sean asked.

Marlon thought of his cel phone, no doubt looking like a piece of Swiss cheese in the front seat of his van.

"We're going to get to a phone, and I'm gonna call the DIA, that's what! They'll get these goons off our backs . . . hopefully," Marlon added. "We need some gas, too."

"What about Mom?" Ross asked. "What would your people do with Mom?

"I'm not sure, Ross. To be honest, I don't think they'll even believe me—no offense, Kira."

"None taken," she replied.

"How are we gonna get Dad back?" Ross asked.

"I'm not sure of that yet either, Ross."

High above them, a dark shadow slid through the night sky, blocking out the stars, gliding in absolute silence.

Once again, an ominous shadow fell on their vehicle and kept pace, undetected.

Ross knew of a 24-hour convenience store near the main highway that had gas pumps and a phone, plus sodas, chips, and gum. It was a pretty new Quicky Mart with a soft-serve machine and a 12-flavor drink bar.

And it was very public. It was in full view of the highway, so people would see if something funny was going on.

"Sounds perfect," Marlon said.

"Won't they catch us if we stop? Won't they come after us?" Ross asked.

"No. Like I said, they want us to think

they're gone. They need us to lead them to Kira. We'll be fine if we stop—as long as they don't find out we have an alie—er, off-world guest on board."

11:45 pm - Quicky Mart off of Highway 51

The observatory van pulled up to the gas pump island with only two witnesses present: one, a nervous night clerk; and two, a craft that drifted like a black, metallic cloud of doom so far overhead, no one could see it.

Marlon stepped out of the van and went to the pumps. He pulled the nozzle from its cradle and yawned. Normally, by this time he would have been so tired that he would have dozed off in the middle of any number of late shows. Those were the nights, of course, he wasn't chauffeuring an alien around.

An alien!

Marlon's eyebrows shot up as he raised his head. His eyes popped wide open again.

He had an alie—

"HOW YA DOING?!" a loud voice crackled.

The voice startled Marlon so much he accidentally pulled the hose out of the tank, gashing the side of the van.

He shook his hands in frustration and disgust.

"Give me twenty bucks worth!" he angrily shouted into the speaker above the pump. He shoved the hose back into the tank and flipped the lever to 'On'.

Nothing.

"Sorry, you have to pay first, sir," the voice crackled. "Credit card at the pumps or cash inside."

Marlon rolled his eyes and then opened the passenger door.

"Okay. I'm going inside. Keep your eyes open for anything suspicious. Whatever you do, stay in the van. We can't risk you being seen," he nodded to Kira. "I'll be right back."

Sean watched Marlon walk across the lot to the brightly-lit store.

He then looked into the back, at the alien. A real alien! She and Ross were still sitting together, as close as possible. His *stepmother*. He'd never done that with his own stepmother—and *she* was human. He wasn't even sure if he could.

He spoke hesitantly, unsure whether or not to bring it up. "Kira? I don't know if I should

84

even ask—but how did you meet Ross and his dad? I know it's probably none of my business, but I want—no, I *need* to know. How did you become, you know, so close?"

Kira's eyes were shining like violet penlights in the dark interior of the van. Her body glowed a faint green through her clothes, the honeycombed cells outlined beneath the translucent skin.

"There were two of us, guests of your government. Part of an ongoing cultural exchange program since your 1960s when we first met in deep space by means of your SETI signals. Our cultures were similar enough for mutual benefit, so we established communications on an ongoing basis. Many of us were chosen, thousands actually, to participate.

"I am what you would call a social anthropologist. I looked forward to the exchange, as I was extremely interested in your cultures. Although my culture may have a few more technological advances, Earth's social systems and relational interactions are far richer and more complex than our own. I felt we could learn so much from you. We wanted to understand your feelings—your emotions.

"We were promised placement in 'foster homes'—human families to live with so we could experience your cultures first-hand. We were promised public indoctrination through schools and other educational facilities. We were promised that diplomatic ties would be established on all fronts and in all nations.

"We were promised a lot."

She tussled Ross' hair and smiled.

"In the end, we were shown defense installation after defense installation. We enjoyed the fine cuisine of your military cafeterias, saw most of your country through blackened windows and from Air Force jets. Not exactly what we had in mind.

"Some of us realized that our dreams of integration were not to be realized, so we took it upon *ourselves* to experience your world, your people. A few of us looked for a chance to escape our 'diplomatic responsibilities'.

"For myself and my partner, our chance came when the vehicle we were being transported in, crashed on your Highway 51. The driver and guards were killed instantly. I wanted to run, to seize the opportunity to do what I came here to do. My partner refused. He thought it best to wait for the proper authorities and continue with the project the way it was going.

"I ran.

"Throughout the next year, thanks to the kindness of Al Clemens, I stayed hidden in a secret room at the Al-e-inn. Eventually, he introduced me to some of his friends.

"That's how I met Richard Hall and his son, Ross. Al arranged for me to spend a month with them. They accepted me as a 'foster guest' despite our vast differences, and believe me, there were plenty. In fact, Ross was terrified of me at first."

Sean looked at Ross, then Kira.

"Did—Did you ever fight?"

"Oh, yes. There were fights. Many fights on many occasions. Some about silly things, some about serious things. They were helpful. We learned a great deal about each other. We're not a perfect family—but then, who is?

"And we will remain a family, *regardless* of what happens."

Sean and Patricia didn't say anything. They felt badly about their initial reaction to Kira. She was as "human" as anyone else they had ever met.

Sean turned to look toward the store, watching Marlon use the payphone and pace back and forth as far as the cord would allow.

No one saw the black sedan pull up to the corner of the lot.

"I'll wait all night if I have to, so you might as well get him on the line *now!*" Marlon yelled into the phone. "This is a serious situation . . . No, I will NOT leave a . . . I can't say over the phone . . . Look, just tell him it's Marlon Walker, and it's a matter of national security!"

Muzak. Then a disconnection.

Marlon throttled the phone.

Then he saw the black sedan.

The phone dropped from his hand.

"Oh, no. NO!" he cried.

Three men in black suits were running across the lot, sneaking up on the van from behind, weapons drawn.

They had seen. They knew. They knew she was in the van! "Get out of there! GET OUT OF THERE!" he yelled, running for the front door of the store.

Sean saw Marlon's frantic motions and looked into the side view mirror on his door. He saw MIBs running toward the van and panicked!

"OH, MY—THEY'RE HERE! THEY'RE COMING! RUN!"

The passenger door flew open. Sean scrambled out, tumbled to the pavement then rolled to his feet.

Patty, Ross, and Kira pushed the side door open, jumped out, then scrambled between the pumps, heading for the store.

As the men started to aim their weapons, their brains registered: *gas pumps*. They thought better of it.

Kira was the last one to the store's door. Before entering, she turned—and pulled a phaser from under her shirt. Expertly, she fired a brilliant blue bolt into each man, sending them all sprawling unconsciously to the pavement.

Three more black sedans pulled into the lot.

More were coming, she was sure of it.

She backed into the store.

The clerk looked at her in panic, shrieking in terror. He reached frantically below the counter—

She fired without even thinking about it. The bolt hit the clerk dead-on, sending him sprawling to the floor.

"WHAT'D YOU SHOOT HIM FOR?!" Marlon bellowed.

"I thought he was going for a weapon!"

"Great! *There's* a headline if I ever saw one. 'Cashier claims: I was shot by a space alien!' "

Beneath the counter, right above the unconscious cashier's head, a red light—a silent police alarm—began to flash.

Marlon took one look out front, counted the number of MIB agents, then doubled it to include the agents he figured were already at the back of the store. They were surrounded.

"That's it," he said, dropping his arms to his sides. "We're trapped."

Outside, one black sedan arrived later than the others.

It parked across the street from the store, away from the other cars, so far in a ditch that the bushes on the side of the hill were pressed against the passenger window. Linda Weber looked at the storefront, counting the number of MIBs on the front and side lots. She was monitoring their communications as the helicopters came sweeping in.

She raised a scramble-protected cellular phone to her ear and dialed a number, never taking her eyes off the store.

"Hello? Howard Phillips?" she asked. "Hi, this is Linda Weber . . . Yeah. You still looking for a meaty story on all that kooky UFO stuff?"

15

12:30 pm - Quicky Mart off of Highway 51

"What are we gonna do now?!" Patricia cried, crouching in the middle of the snack chip aisle.

After the MIBs had pulled their unconscious members to safety, they issued the command for everyone to come out with their hands held high. Marlon yelled again to them that he was DIA, and again, it apparently didn't matter.

Marlon then told everyone in the store to stay down until he could figure out what to do.

"Can't we call the police or something?" Patricia asked frantically.

"I don't think we'll have to," Sean moaned. He had been peeking around the lottery ticket machine, watching the MIBs as they gathered around their vehicles and trained their weapons on the store. It was then that he noticed the first police car arrive.

The local sheriff.

Then two deputy cars pulled up.

They had come in response to the silent alarm, expecting a hold-up at the very worst. They hadn't expected this.

The moment they stepped out of their cars, they were pulled aside by official MIB goons holding up ID badges.

Sean couldn't make out exactly what was being said, but judging by the sheriff's red face, it wasn't a pleasant exchange.

Then Sean saw the sheriff yell and thrust a fat finger into one of the goons' chest while two of his buddies blocked the deputies from getting any closer to the front of the store.

"They won't let local law enforcement get involved. Period," Marlon said from behind the front counter. "They can't afford to. They can't risk anyone seeing Kira."

He reached down and checked the cashier. Still unconscious. "All right, I don't get it. That weapon punched holes in my van like it was tinfoil, but this guy doesn't even have a mark on him. Why?"

Kira and Ross were crouched at the end of the paper product aisle, right across from the main counter.

"It's the latest model in a line of 'smart' weapons your military developed using our technology. It can tell if a target is organic or inorganic and adjusts the intensity of the beam accordingly."

"You mean, that weapon is *ours?*" Marlon asked with astonishment.

"Not just your country's. They're in fairly common use now, worldwide. At least in certain circles."

Marlon growled, "I'll bet that's not the *only* thing, is it?"

Before Kira could answer, Sean shouted, "There's a reporter out there! He's got a mike and a camera and everything!"

Marlon peeked through the window from behind the Havoline Motor Oil sign unable to believe his eyes.

There *was* a reporter.

It looked like the coughing guy from the UFO lecture. He and his cameraman were being harassed by the MIBs, including a lot of shoving, pointing, and yelling. A reporter! This couldn't get any worse. The MIBs would have to end this quickly. Any chance of news coverage was the worst-case scenario for—

He saw not one, but two other news vans roll up, ready to cover the mayhem.

"We are in serious trouble here."

"Your people at the DIA. What did they say? Can they help us?" Kira asked.

"I couldn't get through. It doesn't matter now, anyway. By the time they could help it wouldn't matter. Those MIBs are going to have to get you out of here *now*. It's all they can do to keep the sheriff and his deputies in check. Now two other news crews are out there. We're all about to be caught in a major media event."

Outside, the first cars were slowing down and stopping, full of curious on-lookers and locals gathering to check out the big scene at the Quicky Mart.

One of the MIB threw his hands up in the air in frustration.

"Mr. Walker," Sean said, "maybe this isn't such a bad thing."

"What do you mean?"

"What if Kira goes public?" Sean asked,

unconvinced himself whether or not it was a good idea.

"What?" Patricia cried. "That's nuts!"

"Seriously. What if she walks out there? They can't just shoot her in front of all those people. All those reporters. All those cameras."

"Hmmm." Marlon thought about it. The kid had a point.

"They're gonna get us out of here anyway. At least this way everyone would know the truth. At least she would be safe. Other agencies will want to talk with Kira. Everybody will want to know how this all happened. Is she really an alien? With that kind of crowd, they couldn't hide her or keep her a secret any longer."

Marlon thought about it long and hard. No one said a word as he rubbed his face and weighed the options.

"I'll go first. I'll hold up my badge and let everyone know I'm a federal agent. You come behind me, Kira. We'll go slow—"

"NO!" Ross shouted. "They'll just take her away. If it isn't them, it'll be someone else. I'll never see her again! *I'll* tell them about us! I'll tell—"

No one expected it, so no one reacted.

Ross jumped to his feet and started to run toward the door.

"ROSS, NO!" Kira shot to her feet behind him, reaching out and grabbing his shirt collar.

Marlon heard the shot before he had made it halfway over the counter. He never even saw the metal rack that put a good-sized dent in his head and sent him sprawling to the floor.

Ross heard a sound like thunder as the wall of glass before him blew out.

The hand that had gripped his collar so firmly a split second before, fell away.

Outside, behind the cover of a black sedan that had been pulled in front of the gas pumps, a shaken MIB agent learned the hard way that even alien technology wasn't fool-proof. The beam had misfired. It hadn't adjusted its intensity. It shouldn't have torn through the woman the way it tore through the glass.

Inside, a DIA agent lay unconscious on the floor of the convenience store amid a fallen rack of candy and gum, two screaming kids kneeling close by.

A young boy crouched over his step-mother, crying and staring in shock at the smoking hole in her shirt, surrounded by a growing magenta-colored stain.

16

The crowd was just getting over the shock of the blast when a voice came over the gas pump speaker. The reporters were the first to take notice, Howard Phillips in particular. He managed to get closest to the speaker before the goons started moving people away.

The voice was cracked and garbled.

"Hello? HELLO?! I'm about to start saying things certain people out there really don't want me to say—"

The reporters and the local law officials glared angrily at Special Agent Kelly. They were amazed that one of the "federally wanted, armed and dangerous felons" was apparently a little boy.

Special Agent Kelly cleared his throat in embarrassment and walked quickly to his car.

He spoke into the radio, tuned to the intercom inside the store.

Kelly's voice came through the intercom.

"Hello? Is this Ross? You gotta listen to me, buddy. That was an accident. A misfire. It should only have knocked her out. That's all. We weren't trying to hurt her. You believe me, don't you, Ross?"

Sean didn't correct the agent on his misidentification. He steadied his nerves, crouched behind the counter, and spoke. "She's hurt bad. Real bad. We have to get her out of here now!" He released the button on the side of the mike.

"Well, that's what we want, too. But we have a little bit of a problem. I know you've seen the crowd out here. We've gotta be discreet about this."

Sean pressed the button again. "I'm listening."

"Well, some of these guys are trained to know what to do with her, um, *unique* structure, so what we'll do is send in a med team. They'll put her on a stretcher and hide her face so they can get her out of here. So you sit tight and don't let any of your friends in there do anything.

We'll escort all of you to safety." Kelly's men were already putting together a stretcher they'd taken from the trunk of one of their black sedans.

Sean put the mike down and crawled around the counter.

"I don't know what to do."

Ross was crying harder, holding his mother's hand. The honeycomb-like cells of her skin opened and closed rapidly, as if gasping for air. Her eyes were closed, and the stain on her shoulder was growing larger by the second.

"Mr. Walker's out cold," Patricia said, on the verge of tears. "It's just us, Sean. It's just us! What are we going to do?"

"We-We're going to have to let them come and take—"

"NO!" Ross cried. "*We* have to get her out of here! Away from them!"

"And go where, Ross? Our house? Mr. Walker's house? No place is safe! We don't have any—" Suddenly, an idea struck Sean.

He quickly felt around in Marlon's pockets, searching for a business card——the one he had received while standing at Vance's table at the seminar.

The card had Linda Weber's phone number—her mobile phone number.

The phone on the seat beside Linda rang. She kept her eyes on the escalating developments in the front of the store as she picked it up. "Linda," she answered.

"Ms. Weber! It's me, Sean. Kira's been shot! I think she's dying! You gotta help us! If they take her, Ross'll never see her again. They should be together. They're a family. Please!" Sean crouched low in the back hallway near the storage closet and the restroom—as well as the back door marked 'FIRE EXIT'.

"Sean, calm down. Where's Mr. Walker?"

"He's out cold."

"Are you on a pay phone in the store?"

"Yes."

"Give me the number."

Sean read the number listed on the phone and nervously told it to Linda.

"Okay, Sean, listen to me. I'm right outside in a black sedan. I'm going to pull around behind the store. When I call back, you're going to get everyone into the car, okay? Can you, Patricia, and Ross manage everyone?"

"Yes. We can."

"Okay. Be ready in a couple of minutes."

She hung up the phone and double-checked the MIBs' positions around the store, which she had plotted on her notepad. Then she scribbled another note.

Linda picked up the phone and called two people.

The first was Vance Lewis.

She gave him the approximate time and location for a once-in-a-lifetime opportunity to test his favorite pet project. He eagerly accepted.

The second call was to someone she had never actually met face-to-face.

He was a man who owned an airstrip, Wrights field. It was off the alien highway, about twenty miles away. On occasion, he had helped her with "out-of-towners" who needed rides to safety. She told him to have a plane ready and to wait for a black sedan. He agreed.

At the gas pumps, a boy's voice once again came through the speaker and told a certain MIB official to take a hike and not to come anywhere near the front of the store.

Linda hung up the phone and took a deep breath. There was no going back now.

This wasn't her fault, she said to herself.

They'd lied to her. They deserved it.

Sean is right, she thought. That woman is Ross' mother, whether she's from Fairfield or from another planet. They love5 each other as much as any family could.

She leaned over, opened the glove compartment, and pulled out a peculiar-looking weapon. It was a design which—to her best recollection—had never had a recorded misfire until tonight.

She flipped a small switch on its side and hoped the misfire was an isolated incident.

17

They waited on pins and needles, staring at the phone, waiting for it to ring.

Ross sat by his mother, wishing her eyes would open. He wanted so desperately for that limp hand to suddenly tightly grip his own. He wanted to hear her melodic voice tell him everything was going to be fine.

Patty and Sean waited by Marlon. Once they received the signal, they would grab him around the waist and ankles, and haul him out.

"Sean, he's heavy! I don't know if I can do this," Patricia muttered.

"Yeah, you can. But that reminds me," Sean said, reaching around to gather up some of the candy that had spilled from the fallen rack. He shoved a handful into Marlon's jacket pocket, then threw some money down in payment.

"Mr. Walker will thank me when he wakes up."

The phone rang.

Sean scrambled to answer it quickly, grabbing the receiver with a trembling hand.

"Hello?!"

"Sean," Linda said, "come out, NOW!"

Sean and Patricia grabbed Marlon and moved him as quickly as they could. He was much heavier than they thought he'd be. Patty was huffing and puffing by the time they dragged him through the back door.

Linda Weber stood waiting for them in front of the opened rear door.

Sean noticed she was holding a powered-up alien phaser. Then he saw a formerly concealed MIB agent draped across a nearby rock. She must have taken him down with the phaser, he thought. He was sure there were others nearby.

"Go! Hurry! You have to be gone before the next radio check-in! You have about three minutes!" Linda whispered.

With Marlon placed in the backseat, Sean and Patty ran back inside the store.

Linda watched them bring Kira out and saw her condition. She felt her heart sink. Kira's condition was worse than she'd thought. The back of her shirt was soaked. Her skin color had turned greyish-blue.

"Ross, you'll find a pad in the backseat. The pad is coated with a light-green gel. I want you to hold it on the wound. Hold it by the metal handle on the back, and don't let the pad touch your skin. Understand?"

Ross nodded as they placed Kira in the back seat with Marlon. Ross crawled in and closed the door.

"Patty, Do you know where Wrights field is?"

Patty nodded, too nervous to speak.

"Get there as fast as you can, and don't stop for anyone or anything!"

Patty nodded, climbing into the driver's seat with a look of growing dread.

"Sean, take my phone. When you get about halfway to the field, I want you to dial two numbers. The first is pre-programmed into memory one. The second is in memory two. When you call the first number, a man will answer. He's a special, um, consultant, on these types of projects. Read the first part of this note to him. Read the remainder of the note to the second person you call."

Sean looked at her in disbelief. "You're not coming with us?"

"I can't. Now, go! They're radio-checking now!"

Sean jumped into the car as Patty turned the ignition switch.

As the car turned the corner of the store, Linda ran to the unconscious agent stationed furthest from the rear of the store (whose radio was indeed crackling with a voice saying, "position 4, check-in").

She repeated her alibi in her head, just to be safe. "I knew I shouldn't have been that close to the scene, but I was hoping to assist. Unfortunately, I was surprised by the alien, just like the rest of the MIB agents. I was taken down. They took the car by force and escaped."

She held the phaser at arms length, then turned it on herself. Her finger found the trigger switch.

Again, she hoped the misfire that had torn through Kira was an isolated incident.

Fortunately, it was.

18

Special Agent Kelly saw the car swing out from the side of the store. He felt angry enough to toss his hairpiece to the ground, even though the car was one of theirs.

"Who authorized that vehicle to be anywhere near the rear of the store?" he barked at the closest agent. The agent shrugged.

"Sir," another agent called, "we're not receiving a position check from any of our personnel at the back of the store."

Kelly looked at the unauthorized car once more as it tore onto the highway.

"It's them!" he yelled.

Then he noticed Howard Phillips standing at the front of the reporters, just waiting to overhear something meaty.

He spit through his teeth and walked over

to the black sedan with the gold seal on the license plate. The window cracked ever so slightly.

"It was them." He would have offered a suggestion, but knew all too well that his opinion mattered very little to the shadowy figure seated inside.

The voice was cold and unforgiving. "I've authorized use the of Dark-Cloud. By doing so, we are risking a second sighting, a verifiable UFO encounter. I expect you to arrange the necessary cover story to avoid that possibility. Debrief the media and the police, then go home."

Kelly knew he had failed. They didn't like to use Dark-Cloud in this manner. It was embarrassing to the entire project. He would end-up taking the rap.

Now he had to come up with a cover story and see it through. Lots of paperwork. Lots of calls. Lots of follow-up. A downed satellite would be good, he supposed.

But where would he get a satellite at this hour?

He approached the crowd as the black sedan with the gold seal drove off.

Patty watched the rear view mirror in a

state of paranoia that would have made Marlon proud, only he was still passed out on the back seat.

Sean studied the road ahead. The twisting, mountainous stretch of highway was dark, with only an occasional connecting road and street light. The brightest lights shone on the green signs hanging from the overpass bridges. He was scanning for the one that would read "Wrights field Airport."

Ross held the medical pad to his mother's shoulder. The wound had stopped bleeding, but she still hadn't opened her eyes. The whole pad felt hot. He could tell by the light escaping at the edges that the area beneath it was glowing a blinding white.

"Watch for the exit, Sean. I can't even concentrate. I'm so scared! I just want to go home," Patty cried.

"So do they," Sean remarked, reading Ms. Weber's note.

"We're about halfway. Go ahead and call," Patty remarked nervously.

Sean picked up the phone and hit the first preset number. He waited nervously, butterflies growing to bats in his stomach. He thought his heart would explode when a low voice answered.

"Yes?"

"This is—never mind. Listen, we're on our way to Wrights field, where we're gonna have ourselves a press conference. That is, if Ross' dad isn't there waiting for us. No MIBs. Got it?"

The man on the other end was silent for a moment, making Sean nervous.

"Fine, Mr. Edwards. I'll see you there—if something unexpected doesn't come up. Give my best to Patricia."

Sean gulped as he hung up.

He then punched in the other number.

"Who you calling now?" Patty asked.

"It's on the note," Sean said. "Hello? Mr. Phillips? You the reporter? I'm calling on behalf of Linda Weber . . . Yeah. She wants you to bring as many people and reporters and cameras as you can to Wrights field Airport right away . . . Oh, yeah. Yeah . . . that *was* me on the gas pump speaker . . . Oh, yeah? No, I'm twelve.

Howard had such a coughing fit that Sean had to hold the phone away.

"Whoa. You should see a doctor about that. Yeah, you bet there's a meaty story here. Let's just say you'll see someone very special take off. See you in a few . . . bye.

"We're set," Sean said.

A light in the rear view mirror suddenly grew so bright, it nearly flooded the car.

"Whoa!" Sean cried in surprise.

"What?" Patty asked, turning her head to look.

Then she wished she hadn't.

19

It was hovering behind them, about three feet above the road.

Sean guessed the object was fifty feet wide. It was definitely shaped like a manta ray with metallic black skin and rippling white lights.

"SEAN!" Patty screamed. She lost control of the car for a moment, jerking the wheel from side to side.

The left side of the car brushed the concrete divide wall. It screeched loudly and sprayed a sheet of white-hot sparks.

It's just like Vance's model, only much larger—and functioning! Flying right behind us! Sean thought. They were through messing around. They were going to get Kira one way or another.

Sean draped over the seatback and shook

Mr. Walker as hard as he could, shouting at the top of his lungs.

No good.

The saucer surged forward, skipping in the air as if it was on water. It seemed to be riding the intense orange field that surrounded it. It drifted from side to side, lining itself up perfectly with the rear of the car. Two small red lights surged to life on posts jutting out from its front.

Cannons, thought Sean.

"ROSS! KIRA'S PHASER!" Sean yelled. "Throw it to me!"

Ross did so, carefully keeping the pad on his mother's wound.

The saucer surged forward again, as if to compare its own massive size with that of the car. Sean could actually make out the details of its etched surface, which now filled the rear windshield. If it's trying to scare us, thought Sean, it's doing an excellent job.

"FLOOR IT!" Sean yelled.

Patty pushed the accelerator all the way down. The speedometer climbed past seventy, seventy-five . . .

The trees and road signs flew past in a

blur. For a moment, Patty thought she saw a Wrights field sign. She hoped it was just her imagination.

The saucer backed off slightly and did a full roll, staying even with the car, hovering over the road.

"What's it doing?" Patty shrieked. "What's it DOING?!"

"It's showing off," Sean yelled. He flipped the power-up switch on the phaser.

The saucer took off, pulling straight up and disappearing.

"Where did it go? WHERE DID IT GO? SEAN, DO YOU SEE IT?!" Patty yelled.

"Yeah," Sean remarked softly, watching the craft descend.

It was now hovering right in front of them, flying backward as the car's speedometer hit eighty-five.

The cannons on the front of the saucer began to glow green.

Sean placed his finger on the electric window switch on the door.

"SEAN!" Patty cried, feeling a sudden rush of air from outside.

By the time Patty realized what he was

doing, Sean had leaned hard into the door with his arm thrust in front of him through the open window. He felt a moment of doubt.

Then fired.

The beam hit the saucer dead-on. A shower of metal bits and fire rolled off, pouring down on the hood and across the windshield. Sean felt his hand get singed as he yanked it back inside. He slid across the seat into Patty.

Everyone screamed as they looked through the windshield. It looked as if they were flying through a firestorm.

Then the road appeared again.

The saucer was gone.

"WHERE IS IT?" Sean yelled.

"BEHIND US AGAIN!" Patty cried, jerking the wheel hard to the left to take the curve, the car threatening to turn over.

Ross barely managed to keep the pad on his mother's wound. "CAREFUL! BE CAREFUL!"

"IT'S WRIGHTS FIELD!" Sean yelled, rolling up his window.

The saucer dropped low to the road, lurched slightly, then fired.

The cannons belched a thick stream of green light onto the road, exploding into running fireballs, tracing the car up each side.

The kids screamed. The heat was unbearable as the car's interior glowed bright orange!

Then the cold blue of the night and the winding road appeared again, along with the overpass and exit marked "Wrights field Airport."

"That was a warning not to take aggressive action again," Kira moaned in a barely audible whisper.

"MOM!" Ross cried. Kira's skin began to change from blue-grey to tan. Her eyes began to glow faintly again.

"MOM, WE'RE ALMOST THERE! HANG ON! PLEASE, HANG ON!" Ross' joy was cut short when he noticed the red, green, and blue lights filling the car—a carnival of lights. "No. NO! NOOOO!"

He whipped his head around as a white cone of light hit his eyes, shrinking his pupils to the size of pin pricks.

The saucer had leveled behind the car and tilted back. A small panel had opened on the bottom like a hideous jaw and was emitting a white cone of light.

The car lurched violently.

"NO!" Patty yelled, tugging at the wheel,

realizing the exit was only a few moments away.

The car lurched again, and, suddenly, everyone felt a sense of weightlessness.

Ross knew what was happening. He had felt it before, in the bushes above the trailer, when his feet had left the ground. This time, he feared, there would be no sudden glitch. No sudden mechanical error to allow an escape. No time to hide from blinding search lights.

He closed his eyes as the car began to leave the ground.

Patty desperately kicked and clawed her foot at the brake, as if it would somehow stop the terrifying assault.

"TRY THIS ON FOR SIZE!" a voice shouted over the radio.

"It's Vance!" Sean yelled, "VANCE!"

Vance Lewis felt an extreme rush of adrenaline as he jumped his truck out of the ditch and onto the road, slamming the accelerator to the floor. He couldn't decide if it was from seeing that baby fly or because he was going to test his unemployed friend's device. He laughed outright, then screamed at the top of his lungs.

There was no way he could catch up to them, but that was the beauty of it, he thought.

Just like there was no pilot in that remote vehicle, he didn't have to be near it either.

To send it down.

He pressed the switch taped on his dashboard, sending a current through the wires that snaked through the small sliding rear window to the device in the truck bed. The device, which looked like a mix between a dishwasher and a Radio Shack nightmare, emitted a faint hum.

And an invisible signal.

The saucer lurched violently, like a cow trying to shake away a cloud of annoying flies from its head.

The beam from its belly died, sending the car back onto the road with a bump and a shower of sparks.

"PATTY! THE EXIT!" Sean yelled.

Patty turned the wheel hard to the right, barely making their exit. The car shot up the off-ramp.

The saucer spun out of control—

And smashed into the overpass, exploding into a tremendous ball of fire and rain of twisted metal debris.

The black sedan roared by, crossing the quaking bridge as the last traces of fire in the sky vanished.

Vance skidded to a stop amid the fiery debris strewn about the highway.

He closed the truck door, stepped out, and did the biggest touchdown victory dance ever, on the alien highway.

20

The single-engine Cessna sat on the runway in front of the barn-like hanger. The engine was running, ready for take-off. A man in a flannel shirt and black jeans watched the car approach, then climbed on board the plane.

"There they are," Sean said breathlessly.

A black helicopter, with a gold seal on the side, was parked far from the plane in the grassy field near the small concrete runway.

There appeared to be no one else around.

"Pull close to them," Ross said quietly, holding his mother's hand.

As soon as Patty stopped the car, the side door of the helicopter opened, and a man stepped out. A man with a beard, glasses, and a haggard expression.

"DAD!" Ross yelled, running from the car into the man's waiting arms. Richard's expression exploded into a grin as he lifted Ross from the ground, holding him tightly.

"Your mother, Ross! Where's Kira?" Richard asked hopefully.

"She's in the car. She's hurt, but I think she'll be okay. No. I *know* she'll be okay," Ross said with a smile.

Sean and Patty got out of the car as Ross and his father ran over and leaned inside to see Kira.

A shadowy figure, dressed in a black suit, emerged from the opened side door of the helicopter and walked gracefully toward them.

He was flanked by two guards in similar suits. One was carrying a stretcher.

Sean and Patty felt their knees begin to buckle when they saw him. Sean's mind raced for something to say.

The shadowy figure walked right up to them, the two guards staying a few feet back.

The figure looked down at them with glowing violet eyes, and extended a honeycomb-scaled hand. His mouth turned up in a smile, his skin wrinkling like thin plastic.

"Congratulations, Mr. Edwards. And to you, Ms. Edwards." He reached up to his throat and turned off his electronic voice box, his voice now taking on the strange characteristics of Kira's. "I take it you've already contacted Mr. Phillips. I suppose he and his merry band are on the way. They'll show up at any moment, so I had best get out of here as quickly as possible. Correct?" His tri-level voice sounded dry and a tad smug, but not at all threatening.

Sean nodded in reply.

The alien smiled. "No matter. I've been hoping to bring this situation to a conclusion for two years. And though it didn't end the way I anticipated, you have my appreciation. And thank Mr. Walker . . . Ms. Weber as well. She is a remarkable woman."

Sean wanted to say something, but couldn't think of anything.

The alien walked over to the charred, banged-up sedan and opened a door.

He ignored Ross and Richard, focusing his attention on Kira instead. When he saw her wounded shoulder, he became mildly upset.

"Kira," he said, "you've looked better."

"I'm leaving."

"So I'm told."

The guards reached in and carefully moved her to the stretcher lying on the ground beside the car.

"Kira, you must promise me you won't go public with this for the remainder of your stay on Earth. And when you return home you will say nothing of what has happened."

Kira nodded weakly. "The day will come, you know. The day will come when they will all know."

"Perhaps. But not yet."

They started toward the plane.

"She'll be fine, Mr. Hall. It will take her about a week to recover. She knows what to do."

He turned to Ross.

"You're a brave young man, Ross. Your mother must be proud."

"I am," Kira said.

Sean stopped Ross as everyone else escorted the stretcher.

"Ross, wait! Where are they taking her? Where are you going?"

"Someplace safe. We're not the first to go there, Sean. There have been other off-worlders in situations like Mom's. Some people, like Linda and Al and Vance, have set up places that can help. Waiting stations, so to speak. You see, we'll have to wait about a year for the pick-up."

"Pick-up?"

"Yes. For Mom's friends to come and take her home. Long distance space flight is a pretty big deal where she's from, too—like one of our shuttle launches."

"Wh-What about you and your Dad?"

"We're going, too."

The answer shocked Sean, though he supposed it shouldn't have.

"To another planet?" Sean asked.

"It doesn't matter where we are, Sean. Our home is anywhere we are all together."

He ran to catch up with his family as Kira was loaded onto the plane by Richard and the pilot.

Patty walked over to Sean and put her hand on his shoulder as Ross turned, about to get on the plane.

"HEY! SEAN!"

"YEAH?"

"YOU—YOU WANNA COME?"

Patty's eyes opened wider.

She looked at her brother, as anxious for

an answer as Ross was.

"NAH! SEE YOU AROUND!"

He waved as the plane door closed.

"You mean, you wanna stick around, little brother?" Patty asked. "No more aliens?"

"Yeah. We need to get home, though. I have some packing to do . . . with Mom."

21

A sudden blast of wind got Sean and Patty's attention. They turned and watched the black helicopter take off, the mysterious alien and his guards inside. Sean wondered if he would ever see the shadowy figure or the MIBs again.

Marlon shook his head and moaned, opened his eyes, then realized he was in a car. A car with a black interior. A black sedan.

"BlACK SEDAN! MIBs!" he shouted.

He shot out of the door so quickly, his jacket nearly stayed behind. "Whoa! SEAN? PATTY?" he yelled as they ran back over to him.

With some puzzlement, he saw a small plane taxiing for take-off on the misty runway.

He also saw the vanishing red lights of a black helicopter.

"What happened?" he asked as Sean and Patty ran up and hugged him.

"You're all right!" Sean exclaimed. "YES!"

Sean seemed deliriously happy, Marlon thought. But why? And where was—

"Where are Kira and Ross?"

Sean pointed to the plane.

"And his dad?"

Patty pointed to the plane as it neared take-off speed. Marlon's cheer was as loud as the plane roaring off the runway.

"Okay. So fill me in. What happened after I took the dive?" Marlon asked, putting his hands in his pockets by force of habit, only to come out with a sugar-free 'red-hot'.

"Let's wait for *those* guys," Patty said. "It's a long story, and we don't want to have to tell it twice."

Marlon gave her a questioning look, then noticed the swarm of cars, filled with reporters, locals, and cameramen, pulling onto the field.

"Better save one of those for Mr. Phillips cough," Sean laughed.

"There they go!" Patty yelled excitedly, pointing to the sky.

They looked up and waved at the family whose ultimate destination would be the stars.

About the Authors

Marty M. Engle and **Johnny Ray Barnes Jr.**, graduates of the Art Institute of Atlanta, are the creators, writers, designers and illustrators of the **Strange Matter**™ and **Strange Forces**™ series. They also design **The Strange Matter**™ **World Wide Web page.**

Their interests and expertise range from state of the art 3-D computer graphics and interactive multi-media, to books and scripts (television and motion picture).

Marty lives in San Diego, California with his wife Jana and their twin daughters, Lindsey and Haley.

Johnny Ray also lives in San Diego and spends every free moment with his wife, Meredith.

And now
an exciting preview
of the next

#24 Nightcrawlers

by Johnny Ray Barnes Jr.

1

Bug Begone!—Fairfield's last line of defense against the things that infest us. William Montague, its owner, kept the business open 24 hours a day in case of emergencies. It was easy for him to do this, since he lived in the back of the shop.

Because *Bug Begone!* had a lousy location—a dark side street far off of the main avenue, he almost never got walk ins. His customers got in touch with him by phone.

So when William, who was sitting in his green robe behind his desk, catching the last emotional moments of *Final Jeopardy!* on television, heard someone knocking on the front door at nine-thirty in the evening, he got nervous. He grabbed one of his golf clubs (he still played every other Sunday or so), before going to see who it was.

"Hello?" William asked through the door's glass window. Its shade was pulled and he wasn't about to open it just yet.

"I must speak with William Montague, please," the voice from outside replied. A man's voice. Very sales man-like, but deep. He sounded tall.

William drew up the shade and turned on the

outside light.

The man *was* tall. And pale. Under the light, his pasty white skin took on a yellow, almost rotted tone. He looked to be in his late thirties, and wore a New York Yankees ball cap. He had on a long black trenchcoat, and in his right hand he held a briefcase. William didn't want to consider what might be in it.

It was the man's eyes, however, that kept William from opening the door. The intense stare of the guy—his pupils seemed to grow smaller every second. Nothing this man could say would make William turn that knob.

"I have news about your brother," the man told him. "He's . . . *passed away.*"

William stared at his visitor for some time after that. Neither of them said a word.

"How do you —Who are you?" William asked.

"My name is Whittaker. I was with your brother when he died," the man answered, pupils still shrinking.

Whittaker? William ran the name through his mind and came up with nothing. *This guy could be anybody*, William thought. *He could be lying.*

"How did he die?" he asked.

"It was a rare thing," Whittaker explained. "A bug. A screwworm fly, to be exact. Did you know your brother was sick, Mr. Montague?"

William shook his head.

The man took his eyes from William's and looked around.

"I've driven a long way, Mr. Montague. All the way from Iowa, sir. I would like to tell you about your brother, and it would be nice to do it without a door between us," Whittaker said with a look so honest it had to have been practiced.

"How do I know you're not lying?" William asked.

"Because I know things, Mr. Montague. Last week, your brother sent you a ring in the mail. He told you to keep it a secret."

William blinked. Five seconds later, still gripping the golf club tightly in one hand, he opened the door with the other and stepped back.

Whittaker walked into the shop. He was huge, even taller than William first thought. He could just make out the man's frame under his black trenchcoat. He could tell Whittaker kept in good shape. Under the coat, he was dressed in a sweat shirt, blue jeans and boots.

"So, what happened?" William asked, still not really believing this man's story.

Whittaker sighed.

"Mr. Montague, I believe your chosen profession will enable you to consume this information and comprehend it rather quickly. Are you familiar with the leaf beetle genus *Polyclada*?"

"Yes," William said, remembering the flash cards

he and his partner Barney Lane had made themselves when they first started in the bug business. They'd tried to learn every insect known to man in that first year.

"Well then," Whittaker continued, "you may know that the Polyclada larvae are *highly poisonous*. It's said that the Kalahari bushmen use them to tip their hunting arrows."

William had no patience for this.

"Mister, you just told me my little brother has passed away and now you're giving me a bug lesson? Just get to the point!" William blurted.

"The point is," Whittaker said, "you're covered in Polyclada larvae *right now*. And if you move, they'll crawl onto your skin and inject you with that poison of theirs. You'll be gone before the ambulance gets here."

William froze, his lower lip quivering.

If you move—

He slowly looked down at his green robe and saw that it *was* covered with squirming yellow and black beetle larvae. They clung to the fabric, and their tiny heads wiggled as they gnawed into his nightcoat.

"I know, I know," Whittaker said, circling him, stepping into the shadows, then out again. "At this stage, they don't really resemble beetles, they just look like wet bugs. Their shells haven't fully developed yet, and you can see their bumps and hairs as well as their little black eyes. And—well, the point is, I'm telling the truth here, Mr. Montague. If you move, you're a goner. I think you know that . . ."

William did.

"Wh—When did they—" he stammered.

"Attach themselves to you? Oh, before you even heard me knocking," Whittaker said. "They're excellent in these sorts of missions. Even better than the Navy Seals. Now William, I'm going to ask you the question that brought me all these miles. *Where's the ring?*"

The ring? *William couldn't think, he*—oh, now he remembered—*oh, no* . . .

"I—I don't have it," William choked. "I lost it the day I got the package from my brother! Th—That was three days ago." He could hear noises from the larvae. Awful wet noises.

Whittaker's eyes widened. He pulled down the bill on his cap to hide them.

"Lost it. *Lost it*. Well, I do know it's not here. I could *feel* it if is was. Now where is it Mr. Montague?"

"I put it on the day I received it. It must have fallen off somewhere," William explained.

Whittaker gave a half-laugh then paced once across the floor.

"Your brother tells you to keep the ring a secret so you put it on your finger?" Whittaker asked, his hands shaking. "*Are you the dumbest man on Earth? And you better say yes!*"

"Yes," William squeaked, watching one of the

larvae crawl to the edge of his robe, right at his cuff. It slipped, then caught itself just before it touched skin. Its legs wriggled their way back onto the nightcoat.

"Where might the ring be, Mr. Montague?" Whittaker asked.

William could feel them chewing through, could practically feel their mouths on his skin.

"Any n—number of places. W—We fumigated a few houses that day. And I probably ate at the Steerhunter, like usual. Spent a lot of time in the Bug Vehicle," William said nervously.

"Do you remember *which* homes you went to?" Whittaker asked.

"F—File cabinet back in my office," William's voice trembled.

Whittaker looked back there, then looked back at William and grinned.

"Don't go anywhere," Whittaker said, as he went for the files. As William heard the drawers slam, he could feel his hand cramping from where he held the golf club. He wanted to drop it.

If you move—

"Ah. Here we are," Whittaker said, reemerging into the front room. "You keep excellent files, Mr. Montague. I do so admire an organized person. Now, it seems you did indeed fumigate three houses that day. A Mrs. Helen Moseley, Ivan Brewer, and a ridiculously named family called *the Peels*. And you think the chances are good you lost it in one of these houses, eh?"

William didn't nod.

"Yes," he whispered.

"You know, William, *I think you're telling the truth*," Whittaker said, setting his briefcase up on a counter and opening it. William saw its contents. A cell phone. A notepad. A pen. A full pack of Juicy Fruit. Whittaker tucked the file away inside, then began to walk out the door.

"WAIT!" William squeaked. "What about the beetles?"

"Oh. Yes," Whittaker said, turning to William, who was now drenched in sweat. "SIC 'EM!"

William felt a thousand tiny legs swarm all over his skin, followed by sharp stings *as he rushed out the door for Whittaker*.

The pale man was fast running like a triathlete down the street. William felt his neck numbing as he chased after Whittaker. He coughed as the muscles in his neck tightened and his tongue grew fat. With his eyes watering and his head boiling with fever, dizziness overcame William and he fell hard in the road.

Unfortunately for him, *Bug Begone!* had a lousy location—a dark side street far from the main avenue—and no one would find him for over an hour. When an ambulance finally arrived at the scene, every-one—including William himself—was amazed he was still alive.

GET STRANGE!

Order now or take this page to your local bookstore!

____	1-56714-036-X	#1 No Substitutions	$3.50
____	1-56714-037-8	#2 The Midnight Game	$3.50
____	1-56714-038-6	#3 Driven to Death	$3.50
____	1-56714-039-4	#4 A Place to Hide	$3.50
____	1-56714-040-8	#5 The Last One In	$3.50
____	1-56714-041-6	#6 Bad Circuits	$3.50
____	1-56714-042-4	#7 Fly the Unfriendly Skies	$3.50
____	1-56714-043-2	#8 Frozen Dinners	$3.50
____	1-56714-044-0	#9 Deadly Delivery	$3.50
____	1-56714-045-9	#10 Knightmare	$3.50
____	1-56714-046-7	#11 Something Rotten	$3.50
____	1-56714-047-5	#12 Dead On Its Tracks	$3.50
____	1-56714-052-1	#13 Toy Trouble	$3.50
____	1-56714-053-x	#14 Plant People	$3.50
____	1-56714-054-8	#15 Creature Features	$3.50
____	1-56714-055-6	#16 The Weird, Weird West	$3.99
____	1-56714-056-4	#17 Tune in to Terror	$3.99
____	1-56714-058-0	#18 The Fairfield Triangle	$3.99
____	1-56714-062-9	#19 Bigfoot, Big Trouble	$3.99
____	1-56714-063-7	#20 Doorway to Doom	$3.99
____	1-56714-064-5	#21 Under Wraps	$3.99
____	1-56714-065-3	#22 Dangerous Waters	$3.99
____	1-56714-057-2	Strange Forces	$5.50
____	1-56714-060-2	Strange Forces 2	$5.50

Please send me the books I have checked above. I am enclosing $_____ (please add $2.00 to cover shipping and handling). Send check or money order to Montage Publications, 9808 Waples Street, San Diego, California 92121 - no cash or C.O.D.'s please.

NAME _____ AGE _____

ADDRESS _____

CITY _____ STATE _____ ZIP _____

Please allow four to six weeks for delivery. Offer good in the U.S. only. Sorry, mail orders are not available to residents of Canada. Prices subject to change.

23

JOIN THE FORCES!

STRANGERS™

An incredible new club exclusively for readers of Strange Matter™

To receive exclusive information on joining this *strange* new organization, simply fill out the slip below and mail to:

STRANGE MATTER™ INFO •Front Line Art Publishing • 9808 Waples St. • San Diego, California 92121

Name _____ Age _____

Address _____

City _____ State _____ Zip _____

How did you hear about Strange Matter™? _____

_____

What other series do you read? _____

_____

Where did you get this Strange Matter™ book? _____

_____

23